Joanna Mathews

Uncle Rutherford's Nieces

A story for girls

Joanna Mathews

Uncle Rutherford's Nieces
A story for girls

ISBN/EAN: 9783743372634

Manufactured in Europe, USA, Canada, Australia, Japa

Cover: Foto ©Andreas Hilbeck / pixelio.de

Manufactured and distributed by brebook publishing software (www.brebook.com)

Joanna Mathews

Uncle Rutherford's Nieces

"SUCH WAS THE PICTURE THAT PRESENTED ITSELF TO MY VIEW."—*Page* 10.

UNCLE RUTHERFORD'S NIECES

A STORY FOR GIRLS

BY

JOANNA H. MATHEWS

Author of "The Bessie Books," "Uncle Rutherford's Attic,"
"Breakfast for Two," etc.

"For ruling wisely I should have small skill,
Were I not lord of simple Dara still."

WITH ORIGINAL ILLUSTRATIONS

NEW YORK
FREDERICK A. STOKES & BROTHER
1888

DEDICATED TO

HERBERT HUNT,

WITH LOVING AND BEST WISHES FOR HIS FUTURE YEARS,

ON HIS BIRTHDAY,

AUGUST 6, 1888.

CONTENTS.

CHAPTER I.

AN ARITHMETICAL PUZZLE.

UNCLE RUTHERFORD'S NIECES.

CHAPTER I.

AN ARITHMETICAL PUZZLE.

A SUNNY and a dark head, both bent over a much-befigured, much-besmeared slate, the small brows beneath the curls puckered, — the one in perplexity, the other with sympathy; opposite these two a third head whose carrotty hue betrayed it to be Jim's, although the face appertaining thereto was hidden from my view, as its owner, upon his hands and knees, also peered with interest at the slate. Wanderer, familiarly known as "Wand," — the household dog, and the inseparable companion of my little sisters, — lay at their feet, as they sat upon a low rustic seat, manufactured for their special behoof by the devoted Jim; its chief characteristic being a tendency to upset, unless the occupant or occupants maintained the most exact balance, a seat not to be depended upon by the unwary or uninitiated, under penalty of a disagreeable surprise. To Allie and Daisy, however, it was a work of art, and left nothing to be desired, they having become accustomed to its vagaries.

Such was the picture which presented itself to my view as I came out on the piazza of our summer-home by the sea, and from that point of vantage looked down upon the little group on the lawn below.

But the problem upon which all three were intent had evidently proved too much for the juvenile arithmeticians; and, as I looked, Allie pushed the slate impatiently from her, saying, —

"I can't make it out, Jim : it's too hard. You are too mixed up."

"Now, Miss Allie! an' you with lessons every day," said Jim reproachfully. "Should think you might make it out."

"I'm not so very grown up, Jim," answered the little girl; "and I've not gone so very far in the 'rithmetic; and I'm sure this kind of a sum must be in the very back part of the book."

"Here comes Bill," said Jim, as a boy of his own age and social standing appeared around the corner of the house, a tin pail in one hand, a shrimp-net in the other. "Maybe he'll know. Mr. Edward's taught him lots of figgerin'. Come on, Bill, an' help me an' Miss Allie make out this sum. You ought to know it, bein' a Wall-street man."

Allie said nothing; but I saw a slight elevation of her little head and a pursing of her rosy lips,

which told me that she did not altogether relish
the idea that a servant-boy might possess superior
knowledge to herself, although he might be nearly
double her age. Allie's sense of class distinctions
was strong.

Having faith in his own attainments, however,
the "Wall-street man"—this was the liberal in-
terpretation put by Jim upon his position as office-
boy to brother Edward—deposited his pail and
net upon the ground, and himself in a like humble
position beside his fellow-servant and chum. He
might be learned, but he was not proud by reason
thereof.

"Now le's see, Miss Allie," he said; "what is
it you're tryin' to figger out?"

"It's Jim's sum; and I can't see a bit of sense
in it, even when it's down on the slate," answered
Allie, still in a somewhat aggrieved tone. "He's
as mixed up as a—as a—any thing," she concluded hastily, at a loss for a simile of sufficient
force.

"As a Rhode-Island clam-bake when they puts
fish an' clams an' sweet-potatoes an' corn all in to
once," said Jim.

"*At* once, not *to* once; and they *put*, not they
puts," corrected Allie, who, remarkably choice
herself in the matter of language, never lost
sight of a slip in grammar on the part of our
protégés.

"Seems funny, Miss Allie, that you, that's so

clever in the right ways of talkin', can't do a sum,"
said Jim.

Allie's self-complacency was somewhat restored
by the compliment ; but she still answered, rather
resentfully, —

"Well, I can, a decent sum ! I had five lines
yesterday, and added it all right, too ; but a sum
like that — I b'lieve even brother Ned couldn't
do it !"

That which brother Ned could not do was not
to be compassed by man, in the opinion of the
children. And, as if this settled the matter, Allie
rose from her seat, forgetting for the moment the
necessity for keeping an exact equilibrium, and
that both its occupants must rise simultaneously,
unless dire results were to follow to the one left
behind. The usual catastrophe took place : the
vacant end went up, and Daisy was thrown upon
the ground, the seat fortunately being so low that
her fall was from no great height ; but the rickety
contrivance turned over upon the child, and she
received quite a severe blow upon her head. This
called for soothing and ministration from an older
source, and, for the time, put all thought of arithmetical puzzles to flight ; but after I had quieted
her, and she rested, with little arnica-bound head
against my shoulder, Jim returned to the charge.

"Miss Amy," he said, a little doubtfully, as not
being quite sure of my powers, "bein' almost
growed up, you're good at doin' up sums, I s'pose."

Now, arithmetic was not altogether my strong point, nevertheless I believed myself quite equal to any problem of that nature which Jim was likely to propound; and I answered vain-gloriously, and with a view to divert the attention of the still-sobbing Daisy from her own woes, —

"Of course, Jim. What do you want to know? No," declining the soiled slate which he proffered for my use, "I'll just do it in my head."

"You're awful smart then, Miss Amy," said Bill, admiringly.

But the question set before me by Jim proved so inextricably involved, so hopelessly "mixed up," as poor little Allie had said, that, even with the aid of the rejected slate, it would, I believe, have lain beyond the powers of the most accomplished arithmetician to solve. No wonder that it had puzzled Allie's infantile brains. To recall and set it down here, at this length of time, would be quite impossible; nor would the reader care to have it inflicted upon him. Days, weeks, and years, peanuts, pence, and dollars, were involved in the statement he made, or attempted to make, for me to work out the solution thereof; but it was hopeless to try to tell what the boy would be at; and, indeed, his own ideas on the subject were more than hazy, and, to his great disappointment, I was obliged to own myself vanquished.

"What are you at, Jim?" I asked. "What object have you in all this" — rigmarole, I was about to say, but regard for his feelings changed it into "troublesome sum?"

Jim looked sheepish.

"Now, Miss Amy," broke in Bill, "he's got peanuts on his mind; how much he could make on settin' up some one in the peanut-business, an' gettin' his own profits off it. But now, Miss, did you ever hear of a peanut-man gettin' to be President of the United States, an' settin' in the White House?"

"I believe I never heard of any peanut-man coming to that, Bill," I answered, laughing; "but I have heard of men whose early occupations were quite as lowly, becoming President in their later years."

"An' I ain't goin' to be any peanut-man," said Jim. "I'm just goin' to stick to this place, an' Miss Milly an' her folks, till I get eddication enough to be a lawyer. I find it's mostly lawyers or sojers that gets to be Presidents; lawyers like Mr. Edward. Miss Amy," with a sudden air of apprehension, "you don't think Mr. Edward would try to cut me out, do you? He might, you know; an', bein' older an' with more learnin', he would have the start of me."

"I do not think that Mr. Edward has any ambition to be President, Jim," I answered, reassuringly. "You need have no fear of him."

For to no less a height than this did Jim's ambition soar, and he had full faith that he should in time attain thereto. In his opinion, the day would surely come when, —

> "The Father of his country's shoes
> No feet would fit but his'n."

And it was with a single eye to this that his rules of life were conformed. The reforms which he intended to institute, mostly in the interest of boys of his own age and social standing, when he should have attained to that dignity, were marvellous and startling. No autocrat of all the Russias, no sultan, was ever endowed with the irresponsible powers which Jim believed to appertain to the position he coveted; but, to his credit be it said, these were to be exercised by him more for the benefit of others than for himself.

But he repudiated, now, the idea that the peanut venture upon which his mind was dwelling had any thing to do with his future honors.

"Brother Edward would not be so mean to you, Jim," quoth Allie, who was standing by my knee. "You spoke first to be President, and he would never do such a thing as to take it from you."

"And Jim is not thinking about that when he tries to find out that sum," said Daisy, raising her little bandaged head from my shoulder; "he is quite nice and pious, sister Amy, and wants to do a very right thing."

"'Tain't for pious, neither, Miss Daisy," said Jim, who rather resented the imputation of being influenced by motives of that nature. "'Tain't none of your doin' good to folks, nor any of that kind of thing; it's on'y to animals, cause I'm sorry for 'em."

"O Jim, what grammar!" sighed Allie. For Jim, when excited or specially interested, was apt to lapse into the vernacular against which he and his friends were striving; Allie in particular setting her face against it, and constituting herself his instructress and monitress in grammar and style.

"Can't help it, Miss Allie," said Jim. "Can't keep grammar an' 'rithmetic into my head both to once; leastways, not when the 'rithmetic's such a hard one as this."

The excuse was accepted as valid; and Jim and the matter which was now agitating his mind, both being at present in high favor and held in great interest, any further lapses were suffered to pass without correction or remark.

Jim's love for and sympathy with all animals, especially such as were feeble or disabled in any way, was a well-known trait. A maimed or otherwise afflicted dog, horse, cat, or bird was sure to meet with more favor in his eyes than the most beautiful and perfect of its kind; and he had a horror of shooting birds or other game, which was quite remarkable in a boy of his antecedents. He even questioned the right and expediency of killing animals for food, although he never objected to partaking thereof when it was set before him. Fish, only, seemed to him legitimate prey in the way of sport; and for all noxious insects, snakes, or vermin of any description, he had a perfect hatred, setting at naught the principles of the Society for the Prevention of Cruelty, and really taking a most reprehensible delight in tormenting them, altogether at variance with his feeling for other creatures.

"Bill," I said, turning to that youth as the most practical and clear-headed of the group, "tell me if you know what it is that Jim desires to find out, and the rest of you keep silence, and do not interrupt."

"Well, Miss Amy," answered Bill, "it's just this. Jim was readin' in the newspaper about a' old lady, how she left all her money—an' she'd worked hard for it too, makin' a show of herself on account of bein' so fat—to keep a hospital for all sorts of hurt an' sick animals an' birds; an' Jim, he's just about as much took up with animals an' natur an' things of that kind as she must ha' been, even if he ain't so fat; an' he's got it on his mind to set up his own hospital, an' let Tony Blair an' his sister Matty keep it an' take care of the animals. Tony's lame, you know, and Matty's hunchbacked, an' can't work; so it's kind of beginnin' on the two-legged animals—at least, Tony's only one legged, but he has a right to be two, an' it's a help to them, too."

Poor Tony Blair, with his deformed sister, had formerly been associates and chums of Bill and Jim, in the days when these last had themselves been young vagabonds, waifs, and strays, buffetting with a hard world; and that sentiment in Jim, which was "took up with animals an' natur," had led him to befriend the helpless creatures, and to do them such kind turns as fell in his way. Overwhelming modesty, or a desire to hide his light under a bushel, were not distinguishing characteristics of Jim; but Bill also had borne ample testimony to the fact, that many a time in the old days Jim had deprived himself of a meal — illy come by, it might be — to give it to the little cripples, poorly provided for by a drunken father and ill-tempered mother to whom they were naught but a burden. Many a faded and limp bouquet, discarded by some happier child of fortune, did Jim rescue from the ash-heap and bring to Matty, who had a passionate love for flowers; and not seldom during the spring and summer months would he take a long trudge into the suburbs, and gather wild blossoms to gratify the craving of the little hunchback. On one of these occasions he stole a little, fluffy chicken, which had wandered from its mother's guardianship beyond the garden palings of a small cottage, and, hastily buttoning it beneath his worn jacket, made off as fast as his feet would carry him to bestow his prize upon Matty, who had expressed a longing desire for a bird. But the stolen gift brought naught but distress to Matty's tender heart; for, when the ragged jacket was unbuttoned, the little yellow ball fell lifeless into Jim's hand.

"I'm sure I thought he'd got lots of air to breathe," said Jim, wofully gazing at his victim, while Matty's tears bedewed it; "there's holes enough in my jacket to make it as ventilatin' as a' ash-sifter, an' it was awful mean in him to up an' die on me that way. An', Matty, I wish I hadn't brought him, for him to go an' disappint you like this. Never mind, some day I'll buy you a parrot an' a monkey."

Tearful Matty declined the monkey, but the parrot had long since gladdened her weary hours; for a gorgeous specimen, given to much screaming, even more than is the usual manner of his kind, had been purchased by Jim for her behoof out of his little savings, soon after he and Bill had fallen into good hands, namely, those of my sister Millicent and brother Edward.

This occurred not long after the chicken episode. Milly had become interested in the boys, whom she had encountered at one of the Moody and Sankey meetings, whither they had come, not for purposes of edification to themselves or others, but drawn, partly by their love of music, and partly by the desire to make themselves obnoxious to more decently disposed worshippers. But Milly, by her gentle tact, had disarmed them,

—they being our near neighbors at the service, — and, profiting by this love of sweet sounds, had brought them within her influence; nor ceased her missionary efforts on their behalf until, with the aid of brother Edward, and the consent and co-operation of our parents, she had established them both as servants in the family, where they had opportunity and encouragement to fit themselves for decent and useful lives.

But their rise in life had not caused Bill and Jim to forget their less fortunate little friends and *protégés*, — for Bill, too, had in his way been good to Tony and Matty, though he was not nearly so generous and self-sacrificing as Jim, — and they made them sharers in their improved circumstances so far as they were able. Jim had proposed that they also should be taken into our household, and nursed and cared for; but, as father and mother objected to having the house turned into a wholesale reformatory and hospital, his modest plan was not carried out. Some help, however, had been extended to the two cripples, who could have been provided with good homes in some beneficent institution, could the wretched mother have been induced to give them up; but, thinking probably that they excited sympathy by which she could profit, she refused to do so.

Ever since Jim had fallen upon happier times, it seemed that the boy's whole nature had expanded, and he was constantly on the lookout, to use his own language, "for a chance to do a make-up for all the good done to me an' Bill." A certain ambitious and not unpraiseworthy pride, too, and a strong sense of gratitude and obligation to those who were befriending and helping them, particularly strong in Jim, were causing both boys to make the most of the opportunities offered to them.

And now, it would seem, Jim was actuated by schemes of wholesale benevolence for one, two, and four legged animals.

He had proved himself quite a hero during the last summer; had, through the force of circumstances and appearances, fallen under unjust suspicion, but had been absolutely and triumphantly cleared (the story of which may be found in "Uncle Rutherford's Attic"); and had made himself an object of considerable interest, not only to the members of our own family, to whom he had shown great loyalty and fidelity under severe temptation and trial, but also to outsiders who had known of the story of his adventures. Hence, he had been made the recipient of various tokens of this interest and appreciation, mostly of a pecuniary nature, and he now felt himself to be quite a moneyed man.

With the generosity which was one of his characteristics, — perhaps the most distinguishing one, — he scouted the idea of retaining the whole of his small fortune for his own benefit, pressing

a share of it upon Bill, presenting our children
and his fellow-servants with tokens of his regard,
mostly of a tawdry, seaside-bazaar nature, but
beautiful in their eyes and his own ; conveying,
with an eye to the future, another portion to the
care of brother Edward, to be used for "'lection
expenses" when the time should come for him
to run for that dignity to which he aspired ; and
now it appeared that he had other ends, of a
philanthropic nature, in view.

Old Captain Yorke, a veteran sailor, now retired
from active service, was our purveyor-general,
going each morning in boat or wagon to the
nearest town, whence he brought for us and other
families such supplies as we ordered ; the Point
affording no facilities for marketing or daily household needs.   He was a great friend and crony of
our two young servant-lads, and to him as well as
to Bill had Jim confided his plans ; but the three
heads had proved unequal to the settlement of the
arithmetical difficulties which presented themselves, and Jim had applied to Allie, as being
possessed of greater educational advantages.   This
had not proved equal to the situation, however, as
has been seen ; the knowledge of eight years not
being able to cope with this mathematical problem.

Divested of Jim's complications, Bill's discursive
remarks upon other subjects, and put into rather
more choice English than that in which the latter
delivered it, the plan amounted to this : —

Captain Yorke, heartily admiring, and willingly
co-operating, was to bring from the town a large
quantity of peanuts, which Mrs. Yorke, also full of
sympathy, had promised to roast. The amount
of peanuts purchased was to be determined by the
price per bag, but Jim's ideas were of a wholesale
nature; for my young brothers Norman and
Douglas, who both had a weakness for this vege-
table, had also greatly encouraged him in his
undertaking, giving him not only hopes of great
results from the home-market, but promises that
they would interest "the other fellows," and induce them also to become customers. He was not
to be salesman himself, of course, his daily avocations not permitting of this; but, for the rest of
our stay at the seashore, he purposed obtaining
the services of an acquaintance who belonged in
the place, and who was in the habit of peddling
about papers, periodicals, an assortment of very
inferior confectionery, and other small wares. The
proceeds of these sales made here at the seaside,
deducting a commission for the boy-vender, Jim
hoped would suffice to start his larger and more
ambitious enterprise when we should return to the
city. This was to set up Tony and Matty Blair in
business.

So far all was plain sailing, in anticipation; but
now came the more complicated part of the
arrangement.

A stand was to be secured, a roaster, a fresh

supply of peanuts, and other necessary appliances purchased ; and "our ladies," to wit, mother, Milly, and myself, asked to provide the crippled young merchants with warm clothing sufficient to protect them against exposure to the elements.

There were so many "shares" to be provided for, shares of divers proportions, and Jim's arithmetic was of such a very elementary nature, that he soon found himself lost in a hopeless labyrinth of calculations. With peanuts at so much by the wholesale, and so much at retail, running-expenses, and so forth, on the one hand ; what would be the various amounts to be allowed from the proceeds, on the other, for a "share" for Tony and Matty, another for return profits to Jim's own pocket, and the third and larger for the establishment of the hospital for crippled animals, the main object of the undertaking?

Now, if peanuts were so much per bag, and other needful appurtenances so much more, how much profit might be realized, and what would be the respective shares? Hardly had I solved this complicated problem to Jim's satisfaction, and my own relief, — for, as I have said, numbers were a weariness to my flesh, and the rule of three a burden to my spirit, — when the boy remembered other claimants upon the fund.

"Miss Amy," he said, "didn't I forget. There's Rosie ought to have a share for savin' me out the

Smuggler's Hole ; she *must* have a share, for sure ; an' there's Captain Yorke, he ought to have some, too. Please do it all over again, Miss Amy, takin' out their shares."

This was too much, however, and despite Jim's reproachful appeals to my superior learning, I flatly refused to "do up" any more sums on his behalf.

And now, happily, a diversion in my favor was effected, by the appearance upon the scene of old Captain Yorke himself, who was seen coming up the carriage-way, guiding before him a donkey-cart filled with fish, while upon his arm he bore a basket of fruit, vegetables, and so forth.

He was a character, this old, retired sea-captain, —a firm friend and ally to all pertaining to the names of Livingstone, or Rutherford, or to any belonging to those families, our factotum and stand-by ; and, moreover, an endless source of amusement to the mature part of the household, and of un-bounded admiration to the more juvenile portion. In the eyes of our little girls, and indeed in those of my two younger brothers, Norman and Douglas, and above all, in those of Jim and Bill, he was a veritable hero, for his had been a hard and venture-some life, full of thrilling adventure and hair-breadth escapes ; and the children never tired of listening to the narration of them. Nor, I am bound to believe, did the old man depart from the ways of truth, or draw upon his imagination, in narrating them. But I will let the garrulous old veteran speak for himself, a thing which he was never loth to do.

CHAPTER II.

A CABLEGRAM.

CHAPTER II.

"Mornin', boys; mornin', little ones; mornin', Miss Amy," said the captain, regardless alike of my seniority to the rest of the group, and of any claims of social position over the servants. "Where's pa?" This to me.

"Mr. Livingstone is out driving," I answered, with what I intended to be crushing dignity; for, much as I liked Captain Yorke, it always vexed me to have my father and mother spoken of thus familiarly.

"Ma in, then?" he asked, quite unabashed; and indeed, quite unconscious of any reproof.

"No; Mrs. Livingstone is with Mr. Livingstone," I answered again.

"Wal," drawled the captain, "that's likely enough. If ye see one on 'em drivin' or walkin' roun', you're like enough to see t'other, for they're lover-like yet, if they has got a big fam'ly part grown up. I declar', yer pa an' ma is as like me an' Mis' Yorke as two peas is like two more peas, allus kind of hankerin' to be together, jes' as if we was all young folks yet, an' doin' our courtin'.

Not that pa an' ma is sech old folks as me an'
Mis' Yorke, but they'll get to it bimeby if they
lives long enough."

I passed over the compliment to my parents
without comment, merely asking, —

"Can you leave your message with me,
captain?"

"'Twill keep," he answered; "an' I've got a
bit of business with Jim here. Yer projeck ain't
no secret, be it, Jim?"

"No," replied Jim. "I was just tellin' Miss
Amy, an' askin' her to do up the sums about it;
but"—lowering his voice, and ignorant of the laws
of acoustics, by virtue of which I heard every word
from my position—"she ain't none too smart
at sums if she has had such a lot of schoolin', an'
she didn't make it out real nice and clear like.
But you can speak out. She knows, an' is agree-
ble, an' says she'll help. She's awful generous,
like the rest of 'em, Miss Amy is."

With this little salve to the wounds which my
filial pride and personal vanity had received, he
raised his voice once more, quite unnecessarily,
and continued, —

"Miss Amy, Captain Yorke's got somethin' to
say' bout what we was just talkin' of. Go on,
captain; Miss Amy don't mind."

"I was jes' goin' to tell you what I been an'
done," drawled the old man, raising his hat with
one hand, and rubbing up his grizzled locks with

the other, as was his wont when he was talking at length, — he generally did talk at length when he talked at all. "You've jes' about made up yer mind to do that undertakin', haven't yeou? That peanut-undertakin', I mean."

Jim gave a prompt and decided assent.

"All right. So far so good, an' better too," said the captain, rather illogically; "for if you hadn't, maybe I'd a been a little *too* forehanded, as it were; but it was my opinions you'd made up yer mind for it, so I acted accordin' an' brought 'em along."

"Brought *who* along?" asked Jim impatiently.

"I'm jes' goin' to tell ye," continued the old man. "Don't yeou be in too great a hurry. Things takes time to tell when there's any thin' in 'em worth tellin'; not that I'm no great hand on a long story, for I allers was a man of few words; an' Mis' Yorke she can allers tell a story more to the pint than me, or than any one I know on — bless her heart." — Certainly the old man's loyalty to, and affection for, his dear motherly wife was beautiful to see and hear. — "But she ain't here to tell, an', what's more, she don't know nothin' 'bout it to tell. She ain't the kind to go on talkin', talkin' 'bout things she don't know nothin' 'bout; or, s'pose she does know somethin' 'bout 'em, to go yarnin', yarnin' on forever an' a day, an' never gettin' to the pint, like to Mis' Clay, — ye've seen Mis' Clay, ain't ye? She's Mis' Yorke's cousin, comes over from Millville now an' then, an' the powerfullest han' to talk, an' never comin' to the pint, an' never givin' anybody else the chance."

Mrs. Clay was the captain's pet grievance, and almost the only person of whom we ever heard him speak disparagingly; his objection to her probably being founded on the ground that she never gave him "a chance."

"*Such* a tongue," rambled on the captain, "an' so fast an' confused like she's wuss than the Tower of Babel itself, an' jes' as like to scatter the folks what's livin' around her. But if ye've got a thing to tell that's got a pint, folks mostly likes to hear the ins an' outs of it, 'thout the trouble of askin' no questions, an' I'd as lieve tell 'em to 'em. So I'll tell ye all about it, Jim, an' all of ye."

"Well, if it's any thin' about my business, would you mind havin' it out right quick, Cap?" said Jim.

"An' ain't I a doin' it?" responded the captain. "Don't be in sech a hurry, boy. I got to get my breath to talk, after walkin' up the hill for to rest Sanky Pansy a bit, for the cart was powerful full this mornin', an' he did have a load, an' he's gettin' old an' has to be eased off a bit like myself, an' I felt kind of blowed an' puffy-like. Soon's I can talk good, I will. Young folks is allers got to be impatient. There's my darter, Matildy Jane, she ain't none too patient, you know —

leastways, not onless it's with you, Jim," — here a wink of the eye at Jim made evident the playful irony of the exception, for Jim was Matilda's *bête noir*, and a chronic warfare waged between the two, — "an' she says to me this mornin', says she, 'Pa,' says she, — an' ye might think I hadn't never learned her the Ten Comman'ments, least-ways the one about honorin' her father an' mother; but young folks is different behaved from what they was in my day — at least them's my opinions. I was jest a tellin' her an' Mis' Yorke how Peter Slade got his boat capsized last night; an' 'Pa,' says she, 'it's time my bread was took out of the oven, an' if you've got any thin' to say' — I declar', Miss Amy, if she didn't give me a message about yer clothes; how when the wind riz up last night, some of 'em was carried off the lines into the sand, an' she had 'em to wash over again, an' wouldn't have 'em home jes' up to time. Now, where was I, Jim?"

"Out on the sands, an' upset in Slade's boat, an' talkin' to Matilda Jane; an' where you're goin'. to is more than me or any one else can tell, Cap," answered Jim, saucily. "You started to tell us something about my peanut-business, I believe; but you've got considerable off the line."

"To-o be sure, to-o be sure," said the old man, no whit offended or displeased by the boy's pertness; for the spirit of *bon camaraderie* which existed between them was not easily disturbed.

"Well, now, I'm jes' comin' to it right spang off. Well, ye see, I been over to Millville this mornin' in the boat, accordin' to custom, when the water ain't too rough, an' bein' off extry early, too, for I'd more 'n common to market for, — Mis' Douglas she told me to bring her cowcumbers for picklin'; an' Mis' Stewart she wanted some chany dishes an' some glasses outer the crockery store, — an' that's considerable way from the dock, you know; an' Mis' Yorke she gimme some bit of flannen she wanted matched, — an' such like arrands takes time. So I says, says I, I'll jes' run over to the station an' see what's doin' there, more by token, as it was near time for the express, an' it kind of livens ye up a bit to see them express-trains come in, — they're nice an' bustlin' like, with a sort of go in 'em; an' after she come in, there was a freight-train come, an' there was lots of freight put off, an' — guess what I see, Jim, among it."

"Peanuts, I suppose," answered Jim, "an' I guess I'll get at the whole story jest as quick by guessing it out myself, as by waitin' for you, Cap."

The captain gave Jim a friendly nod, still no whit disturbed by the freedom of his criticisms, and rambled on again, —

"Yes, peanuts, bags of 'em, half a dozen or more, I reckon, though I didn't take the trouble to count 'em; an' the way I foun' out — how do ye s'pose I knew what was in them bags?"

"Smelled 'em," said Jim; "Sampled 'em,"
said Bill, in a breath.

"How was I to sample 'em when they was — I
mean, if they was fastened up in the bags?" continued the captain; "nor it wasn't no smell, either.
There ain't much smell outer peanuts 'thout
they're cookin'. Mis' Yorke, she's a master hand
to roast peanuts, does 'em jes' to a turn, an' then
ye can smell 'em clear down to the beach, an'
fustrate it is, too. I'd rather smell 'em than all
the fine parfumery things they puts up in bottles."

"What about the peanuts?" urged Jim. "Then
how *did* you know, an' what did you do? Hurry
up."

"There was a feller — one of the freight-hands
— a pitchin' of the things outer the cars; an' one
of them bags hit against a barrow stood there, an'
got cut right through, the bag did, — an' what do
you s'pose come a pourin' outer that bag, Jim?"

"Think I can guess that riddle. Peanuts,"
answered Jim.

"Yes, peanuts," said the captain; "an' it was a
lucky thing for Sam Bates, to who they was con-
signed, that there wasn't a raft of youngsters
roun' that freight-house as there is most times
of the day. There's a Sunday-school clam-bake
comin' off up to the Pint to-day, an' I reckon most
of the Millville boys was gettin' ready for to go to
that, so they wasn't on hand. Sam himself was
there, though, an' it beat all, the takin' he was in

over them peanuts ; an', to be sure, it was enough
to make any creetur' mad, to see them good peanuts go rollin' an' hoppin' over the platform, an'
Sam he in a' awful hurry to load up an' go home,
for he's a darter gettin' married this arternoon.
Ye didn't never hear about Sam Bates' darter,
an' her city young man, did ye? Well, ye see,
Sam Bates' darter, her that is called " —

"But the peanuts ; tell us what became of the
peanuts first, Cap," interrupted Jim, determined to
check the old sailor's wanderings, and keep him to
the "*pint.*"

"Why, ye see," meandered on the captain, "when
I see them peanuts a-rollin' round, an' Sam in that
takin', I says to myself, Sam ain't got no time to
lose a-pickin' up of them peanuts, an' maybe he'd
be glad to get rid of 'em for what he give for 'em
an' no profits, an' let Jim have the profits, an' no
freight to pay on 'em but me to get 'em picked up.
'Sam,' says I, as he was fussin' round, 'the Scriptur' says,' — Sam's a deacon in the church, an' I
thought mebbe a little Scriptur' would fetch him,
and keep the price down, — 'the Scriptur' says,
Whatever a man can get, therewith let him be
content ; an' I take it the moral of that is, make
the best of a bad bargain. An' there's another
teks that says, Don't ye fret over spilt milk ; an',
bein' a pillar of the church, I reckon you'd like to
practise 'em, an' let your light shine afore men.'
Now if there's one thing more'n another that Sam

prides himself on, its bein' a deacon, an' livin' up to it ; an' my speakin' Scriptur' to him was jest a word in season, for he quiets down an' falls to reckonin'. 'Give 'em to me for what you give by the lot, an' throw in the freight,' says I, seein' he meant to make on 'em, 'an' I'll take 'em an' see to the pickin' 'em up, an' you can load up the cart an' start off home.' He jes' took to it at once, for, with the lot he had, one bag didn't make so much differ out half a dozen — he buys 'em that way mostly, for ye know he keeps a' eatin' house ; temperance strict it is, up to Stony Beach, where there's lots of clambakes an' picnics holdin' all the time, an' the folks eats heaps of peanuts. So Sam came to my terms, an' I made thirty cents on the bag of nuts, an' the freight throwed in for ye, Jim ; an' me an' Taylor an' Shepherd picked up all the nuts, an' I brought 'em along in a basket Taylor lent me."

Jim turned expectant eyes towards the donkey-cart.

"No," said Captain Yorke, seeing the direction of his glance, "they bean't here in the cart, nor nowheres here ; they're down into the lighthouse. Perry was comin' over in his boat 'thout no load ; an', as I was pretty well filled up, he brought 'em over, an' he's took 'em to his own landin'. Soon's I'm rid of my load I'll go after 'em. Hello !" as a blue-coated, brass-buttoned boy from the chief hotel of the place came running into our grounds, and up to the house. " Hello, here's a telegraph for some on ye ! Hope 'tain't no bad news. I don't like them telegraphs ; ill news comes fast enough of its own accord, an' good news is jes' as good for a little keepin', an' ain't goin' to spile. Mis' Yorke she says " —

But Mrs. Yorke's sayings, valuable though they might be, were lost upon me as I took the yellow-covered message from the hand of the messenger. Telegrams were matters of such almost daily occurrence in our family that the sight of one rarely excited any apprehension ; and, as all of our immediate household were at present here at our seaside home, I knew that the message could bring no ill news of any one of them. But my heart sank as I saw that this was a cablegram, for a dearly loved uncle and aunt were over the sea, and my fears were at once excited for them.

But fear was quickly changed to joy when, opening the cablegram in the absence of my parents, to whom it was addressed, I read these words, —

" We take ' Scythia ' to-morrow for home, direct to you at the Point. All well."

As we had not expected the dear absentees for at least six weeks or perhaps two months, this news was not only a relief, but a joyful surprise, and I gave a little shriek of delight, which called forth eager inquiries from the children, while Captain Yorke and Bill and Jim were alert to catch my answer.

"Uncle Rutherford and aunt Emily are coming home, now, right away; they will be here in a week or so, and they are coming to us, here to this house!" I exclaimed, waving aloft the paper, in the exuberance of my joy.

Daisy forgot her downfall, and her bandaged head, as she and Allie seized one another by the hands, and went capering up and down the piazza in an improvised dance; and Captain Yorke's face beamed, as he said, —

"That's the best news I've heered this summer, leastways next to hearin' Jim was likely to get well that time, for the Pint ain't the Pint when the Governor and the Madam ain't on to it. But, Miss Amy, I wouldn't be for turnin' your folks out afore ye'd go to the city anyhow; for, take ye for all in all, ye're a pretty likely set, an' I'd miss Jim an' Bill a heap."

There was no fear of that: we were tenants for the season in the dear old seaside homestead, where we had been guests for more or less of every previous summer; and the beloved uncle and aunt whose home-coming from a European trip we were now rejoicing over, would, in their turn, be now our much prized and welcome visitors. It would not be for long, however; for, to the great regret of the whole household, our summer sojourn by the sea would in a few weeks come to a close. I said the whole household; but there was one exception, for father had privately sighed all summer for our own country home, where he had his fancy farm, extensive and beautifully cultivated grounds, and superb old trees in which his soul delighted. We told him that a branch of one of these last was, in his eyes, worth the whole broad ocean, in which his family so revelled; and he did not deny the soft impeachment. But his patience was not to be much longer tried, for we were to spend a couple of months at Oaklands after leaving the seashore, and before we settled down for the winter in our city home. Nevertheless, absence from his beloved Oaklands had been more than compensated for by the roses which the invigorating sea-breezes had brought to the cheeks of the two youngest of the household, Allie and Daisy, who had been brought here pale, feeble, and drooping, from the effects of the scarlet-fever, but who were now more robust than they had been before the dreadful scourge had laid its hand upon them.

Nor had the summer been one of unmixed enjoyment, even to those members of the family who gloried in the sea and the seashore; for circumstances had arisen which had been productive, not only of great anxiety and trouble to us all, but which had involved bodily injury, and all but fatal consequences, to poor Jim. And although his name and character had come out scatheless from the trying ordeal of doubt and suspicion which had fallen upon them at that time, it had been otherwise with those of one who had been received as no other than a favored friend and guest in our household; and a young girl whose advantages had outweighed a thousand-fold those of the once neglected waif rescued by our Milly from a life of evil, had gone forth from among us with a record of shame and wrong-doing which had forfeited, not only her own good name, but also the respect and liking of all who had become cognizant of the shameful tale.

To those who have read "Uncle Rutherford's Attic," these circumstances will be familiar; to those who have not, a few words will suffice for explanation.

In the early part of the summer, my aunt, Mrs. Rutherford, had sent to me a pair of very valuable diamond earrings, old family jewels, and an heirloom. They came to me by virtue of my baptismal name, Amy Rutherford, which I had inherited from several successive grandmothers on my mother's side; the young cousin to whom they would have descended, the only daughter of aunt and uncle Rutherford, having died some years since, when a very little girl. She was exactly of my own age; and this, with the fact that she too was an Amy, had caused me to be regarded by my uncle and aunt, especially the latter, with a peculiar tenderness; and they seemed to feel that to me, the only living representative of the family name once borne by their lost darling, belonged all the rights and privileges which would have fallen to

their own Amy Rutherford.   It may be imagined
how I had prized a gift precious, not only for its
own intrinsic value, but for the many associations
which clustered about it.

Scarcely, however, had the earrings become my
personal property, than there followed in their
train such a course of sin, sorrow, and tribulation,
that my pleasure in them was quite destroyed;
and, for a long time, the very sight of them became
hateful to me.

Ella Raymond, a ward of my father's, and a girl
somewhat older than myself, had come to make us
a visit just about the time that the beautiful jewels
came into my hands.   Incited by vanity, and an
inordinate love of dress, this unhappy girl had
recklessly allowed herself to become heavily
involved in debt, — debt from which she saw no
means of escape, and which she was resolved not
to confess to her guardians.   The sight of my
diamonds aroused within her the desire to possess
herself of them, not for her own personal adornment, but that she might dispose of the jewels,
replacing them with counterfeit stones, and so
obtaining the means to satisfy her creditors.

Unrestrained by principle, honor, or the laws
of hospitality, the wish became but the precursor
to the actual carrying-out of the evil thought.
Thanks to my heedlessness, and the careless way
in which I had guarded the earrings, she obtained
them with little trouble ; and after an amount of

duplicity and deceit, terrible and shameful to contemplate in a woman so young, had contrived to carry out her purpose, to have the stones changed, and then to convey the earrings back to my possession, without drawing suspicion upon herself.

Nor, was this the worst; for when, by a most unfortunate series of events, suspicion was forcibly directed toward Jim, she failed to exonerate him by acknowledging her own guilt; and but for the merest accident, which brought about the proverbial "Murder will out" and fixed the crime without a shadow of doubt upon her, would have suffered the innocent boy to bear all the penalties and disgrace which by right belonged to her.

So it will be seen that the summer, spite of its many pleasures and much happiness, had not been without a large share of care and perplexity.

That all this was over, and that our fears for Jim's moral and physical well-being had come to an end, we were most thankful; and the most of us still clung lovingly to the grand old ocean, and our summer-home on its shore.

But autumn gales would, ere many weeks, be sweeping over this exposed coast; and already the summer-guests were flitting from the large hotels, although the cottagers would probably hold their ground for some little time longer. But what would it matter to us if we should be left the very last of the summer-residents upon the Point, so long as dear aunt and uncle Rutherford were to be with us? They were a host in themselves, especially the latter, who always seemed to pervade the whole house with his jovial, hearty presence, and who was the first of favorites with all the young people of the family.

There would be much for them to hear, too : all the sad story related above in brief, to be told, with all its minor particulars ; for it had been kept from them hitherto, as I had been very sensitive on the subject, my own carelessness having been partially in fault, and I had preferred that they should hear nothing of it until their return. Aunt Emily would not have been severe with me, I knew; but I had wished that the face and the voice, which she always associated with her own lost Amy, should speak and plead for my shortcomings in the matter, when it should come to her knowledge. And oh! was I not thankful beyond measure, for her sake, even more than for my own, that the jewels had been recovered, and were once more safe in my own possession, before she learned of the perils they had passed through. If I felt somewhat shamefaced and repentant, as it was, what would it have been if they had been lost beyond recovery!

The joy at the unexpected return of the absentees was not confined to their own family or circle, for the "Governor" — uncle Rutherford had years since held that dignity in the State, and was still "the Governor" to all the denizens of the

Point — was greatly beloved by all who knew him
well; and the old residents of the place, which had
for so many years been his summer-home, considered themselves to be his intimate acquaintances.
He was an authority and a law to each one among
them. What "the Governor" did, was invariably
right in their eyes; from what "the Governor"
said, there was no appeal. He would, indeed, have
been a daring man who should question the right
or wisdom of uncle Rutherford's words or deeds
in the presence of any of these stanch adherents.

And dear aunt Emily was not less beloved in
her way, for the simple people of the Point all
but adored her, — true, wise friend that she had
proved to them; and among them none were more
ardent in their devotion and admiration than
Captain and Mrs. Yorke.

So it was no wonder that the captain's face
beamed with delight, nor that, being somewhat
after the manner of the Athenians of old, who
delighted in some new thing to tell or to hear, he
should now be in haste to despatch his daily business, and take his departure to spread the news
about the Point. Indeed, he would scarcely wait
until I — who regained my senses before it was
too late — furnished him with the list for the next
day's supplies, which mother had confided to my
keeping. In fact, in the midst of the excitement
and pleasant anticipations which uncle Rutherford's cablegram had called forth, Jim's "peanut-

undertakin'" was for the present entirely lost sight of, unless it was by the lad himself and his faithful chum and ally, Bill.

No need to give here the reasons which had influenced uncle Rutherford's unexpected return; they were purely of a business nature, and would interest no one else.

CHAPTER III.

AN ARRIVAL.

CHAPTER III.

I HAD made my confession, — for a confession
I had felt it was, — involving for my own share no
small amount of carelessness, and some little
pride and self-will ; all of which "little foxes" had
opened the way to the commission of actual crime
in another.

It was the day after that on which my uncle
and aunt had arrived at the Point, — mild, soft, and
sunny ; only the September haze upon sea and sky
to tell that the lingering summer was near its end.

We sat upon the piazza, — these two dear new-
comers, my sister Milly, and I. Father off upon
some business ; mother in the house attending to
Norman, who had come home with a sprained
wrist ; the children at play upon the beach with
Mammy, and their faithful pages, Bill and Jim,
in attendance. I had stipulated, with a fanciful
idea that I was making some righteous atonement,
that I should be the one to relate the sad story of
my diamond earrings ; and hence no one had until
now mentioned the subject in the hearing of my
uncle and aunt.

The opportunity was propitious, the audience lenient and sympathetic; and seated on the piazza-step, with my head resting against aunt Emily's knee, and, as the tale proceeded, her dear hand tenderly stroking my hair and cheek, I had told the story to its minutest particular, taking, as the sober sight of after days has shown me, more than the necessary amount of blame upon myself.

So my uncle and aunt now said; and, while inexpressibly shocked at such heartless wickedness in one so young as the guilty girl, they would not allow that their "own Amy" was at all blameworthy in the matter, and only congratulated themselves and me upon the recovery of the earrings. My name, and the likeness I bore to the Amy Rutherford in heaven, would have pleaded for and won me absolution in a far worse case than this; and they at once set themselves to work to demolish my almost morbid fancies in connection with the theft of the jewels. The very fact that I had now told them all was a relief, and my elastic spirits at once began to rise from the weight which had burdened them during the last few weeks.

"So that is the hero of your tale?" said uncle Rutherford, looking thoughtfully down upon the beach where the little ones were enjoying themselves to the utmost, and having matters all their own way, as usual. Jim was lying prone upon the beach, while Allie and Daisy were industriously covering him with sand; Bill assisting by filling their pails for them. This was a daily amusement, and never palled.

"So that is your hero?" he repeated. "And what do you mean to do with him, Milly?" he asked, turning to my sister. "Such a fellow should have a chance in life."

"He thinks he has it since he has been here," answered Milly; "since he has been among respectable people and surroundings, provided and cared for, and taught. He and Bill both talk as if they needed no greater advantages than those they possess already. As to what I mean to do with him, dear uncle, — well, it is less what I mean to do with him, than what he means to do with himself. His own ambitions are soaring, and quite beyond any plans that I could form for him; his aim being the head of the government of our country, with the powers of an autocrat, and no responsibility to any one. Nor is his mind disturbed with any doubts that he will be able to achieve this dignity, provided that he continues to 'have his chance.' At present he is content with learning his duties as a house and table servant, believing those to be but stepping-stones towards his goal."

"To say nothing of his ambitious views regarding Milly herself," I interrupted. But my remark was ignored as unworthy of the gravity of the subject.

"But he should have some schooling, a boy such as he is, — do not you think so?" asked uncle Rutherford; adding, "Whatever his aims and ambitions may be, he can achieve nothing without some education."

Milly hesitated for a moment, unwilling to make mention of all that she was doing for Jim and his *confrère;* and I spoke for her.

"Milly is spending a goodly portion of her worldly substance in that way," I said. "The boys go to a teacher for two hours every evening, and are both making quite remarkable progress in the three R's; and Bill had singing-lessons all last winter, and I believe Milly intends that he shall continue them when we go back to the city."

"H'm'm," said uncle Rutherford. "Very good, so far as it goes; but I mean something more thorough and far-reaching than this." And Milly's eyes lighted, for she knew that uncle was already planning some means of substantial advancement for her *protégé.*

"If you are going to give him any further 'chance,'" I said, "Columbia itself will not bound his ambition. He, too, will sigh because there is but one world for him to conquer."

"H'm'm," said uncle Rutherford again, with his eyes still fixed thoughtfully upon the incipient candidate for presidential honors, who, having shaken himself free from the sand, and risen to his feet, was now tumbling rapidly over in a series of "cart-wheels;" another performance in which the souls of our children delighted, and in which he was an expert. But he — uncle Rutherford — said nothing more at present; and we were all left in ignorance as to what benevolent plan tending Jim-wise he might be pondering.

For a man otherwise so charming and considerate, uncle Rutherford had the most exasperating way of exciting one's curiosity and interest to the verge of distraction, and then calmly ignoring them.

But now I suddenly bethought myself of Jim's "peanut plan," which, truth to tell, had passed entirely from my mind since the day I had first heard of it; and, with an eye to further prepossessing uncle Rutherford in the boy's favor, I forthwith unfolded his scheme for the benefit of the helpless young Blairs. My uncle was amused, but, as I could see, was pleased, too, with Jim's gratitude and appreciation of the good which had fallen to his own lot.

"Amy," said uncle Rutherford presently, — *apropos* of some further allusion which was made to my tale, and to Captain Yorke's share in it, — "Amy, I am going to invite Captain and Mrs Yorke to visit New York this winter, and," with a twinkle in his eye, "shall depend upon you and Milly to escort them hither and thither to see the city lions."

"Invite them to your house?" I inquired, in not altogether approving surprise, for the idea of Captain and Mrs. Yorke as visitors in uncle Rutherford's house was somewhat incongruous ; while the vision of Milly and myself escorting them about was not attractive in my eyes, fond though I was, in a certain way, of the old man and his dear motherly wife.

"Not to my own house, no," answered uncle Rutherford, with an assumption of gravity which by no means imposed upon me, "for I do not expect to have any house of my own this coming winter, — or, I should say, not to occupy my own house ; for, Amy, as my boys will pass the winter abroad, and your aunt and I would feel lonely without them, we have been persuaded by some kind friends, with a whole houseful of troublesome young people, to make our home with them, and help to keep their flock in order. So Captain Yorke and " —

But he was interrupted, as I fell upon him in an ecstasy of delight, — worthy of Allie or Daisy, — enchanted to learn that we were to have the inexpressible pleasure of having him and aunt Emily to spend the winter with us ; a pleasure which I would willingly have earned by any amount of ciceroneship to the old sailor and his wife. The subject had not been mooted before the younger portion of the family, but had been discussed and settled in private conclave among

our elders ; so it was a most agreeable surprise
to each one and all of us.

"But about Captain and Mrs. Yorke?" I said,
at length, when my transports had somewhat
subsided, and calmness was once more restored.
"You do not really mean that you are going to
bring them to the city, and — to *our* house?"

And all manner of domestic and social complications presented themselves to my mind's eye,
in view of such an arrangement. For uncle
Rutherford, in his far-reaching desire to benefit
and make others happy, was given to ways and
plans which, at times, were too much even for his
ever-charitable, generous wife; and which now
and then would sorely try the souls of those less
interested, but who, *nolens volens*, became the
victims of his benevolent schemes.

No one was better aware of uncle Rutherford's
proclivities in this way, or more in dread of them,
than my young brother Norman, who had just
joined our circle, fresh from mother's surgery, and
with his arm in a sling. For Norman's bump of
benevolence was not as large as that of some other
members of the family, and he was inclined to
look askance upon uncle Rutherford's demands
upon his heart and his purse. These, to tell the
truth, were not infrequent ; for our uncle, believing that young people should be led to the exercise of active and unselfish charity, and seeing
that Norman was inclined to shirk such claims,

was constantly presenting them to the boy, with a view to training him in the way he should go in such matters.

"Uncle Rutherford gives with one hand, and takes away with the other," Norman had said, grumblingly, only this same morning, in my hearing.

"You had better say he takes with one hand, and gives seven-fold with the other," said Douglas, resentfully ; for he inherited, to the fullest extent, the family generosity. "Nor, I saw the skins of your flints hanging out to dry this morning."

Whereupon Douglas dodged a book aimed at his head, and left his shot to work what execution it might.

Norman had caught my last words, and taken in their meaning, and his delight at the prospect of a visit from Captain Yorke was almost as great as Milly's and mine in view of the stay of our uncle and aunt at our home; being incited, probably, by the thought of the "jolly fun" which he and Douglas could extract from the old man while piloting him about the city.

"I certainly do not intend to bring the old people to your house, Amy," said uncle Rutherford; "but your aunt is anxious that Mrs. Yorke should see some good physician, who may be able to relieve her from her lameness before she is entirely crippled ; and we shall therefore propose that they come to the city after we are fairly settled there, when we will provide comfortable quarters for them, and put Mrs. Yorke under proper treatment. There is a fitness to all things, my child; and Captain and Mrs. Yorke would probably feel as much embarrassed as your guests, as we should be in having them with us."

"I was only thinking" — I began, then stopped.

"You were only thinking that your quixotic old uncle was about to inflict a somewhat trying experience upon you," said uncle Rutherford, in answer to the unspoken thought. "But he has a *modicum* of sense left yet, Amy."

Truth would not allow me to enter a disclaimer, for this had been my very thought. Any slight embarrassment which I might have felt, however, was relieved by a little diversion in my favor, as uncle Rutherford said, —

"Here is Fred Winston coming over from the hotel."

"Yes, he is generally coming over, and never going back," said Norman, with what I chose to consider a saucy glance in my direction; but I ignored both speech and glance, as I welcomed the new-comer.

Now be it understood, that this young man was neither a gossip nor news-monger; but, being at present a resident of the largest hotel in the place, he was, from the force of circumstances, apt to be the hearer of various items of interest, and these, for reasons which seemed good to himself, he usually considered it necessary to bring over to the homestead as soon as possible after they came to his knowledge. Indeed, our boys basely slandered him, by crediting him with the invention of sundry small fictions as an excuse for coming over to our house. Nevertheless, he was always a welcome guest with each one and all of the family, and with none more than with these saucy boys.

"Mr. Rutherford," he said now, when he had settled himself in such comfort as he might upon the next lowest step to that on which I was seated, and addressing himself to my uncle, who, by virtue of his interest in, and proprietorship of, a great portion of the Point, was regarded by most people as a sort of lord of the manor, — "Mr. Rutherford, have you heard what has befallen Captain Yorke?"

"I have heard nothing," answered uncle Rutherford. "No misfortune, I hope."

Mr. Winston slightly raised his eyebrows, as he answered, laughingly, "I do not know whether he considers it in the light of a misfortune or a blessing; but I know very well how I should feel had such an affliction fallen to my lot, — that it was an unmitigated calamity; while Miss Milly, again, would probably consider it as the choicest of blessings. It seems that the old man had a reprobate son, who, many years since, went off to parts unknown; and his parents have heard nothing of him since, — that is, until to-day, when a woman, claiming to be his widow, appeared with five children. She had his "marriage lines," as she called them, a letter from the prodigal himself to his father, and other papers, which appear to substantiate her claim ; and the old couple have admitted it, and received the whole crowd. 'Matildy Jane' is sceptical, derisive, and *not* amiable. Nor can one be surprised that she is not pleased at this addition to her household cares and labors, for I have not told the worst. The woman is apparently in the last stages of consumption ; one of the children is blind ; another has hip-disease ; and a third looks as if it would go the way its mother is going. There is a sturdy boy of fourteen or so, the eldest of the family, and another chubby, healthy rogue, in the lot ; but they really looked like a hospital turned loose. Brayton and I had gone down for bait, and were talking to the captain, when they arrived."

"Don't, don't, Mr. Winston!" exclaimed Norman. "Milly will adopt the crowd, and have them here amongst us. That is her way, you know."

"And what did the captain say ?" I asked, fully agreeing with Mr. Winston, that this must be, for the old seaman, an appalling misfortune. "Imagine, if the thing is true, and these people dependent upon him, the utter up-turning of the even tenor of his way, — of all their ways. I sympathize with 'Matildy Jane.' What did the captain say ?"

"He asked me to read his son's letter to him, —

for he is not apt, it would appear, in deciphering writing; and, indeed, it was more or less hieroglyphical, — then gazed for a few moments at the dilapidated crew, — dilapidated as to health, I mean; for they are clean and decent, and fairly respectable looking, — and said, 'Well, ye do all seem to be enj'yin' a powerful lot of poor health among ye.' Then he turned into the house, saying that he must 'see what mother said,' giving neither word of welcome nor refusal to admit the claim of the strangers; and presently Mrs. Yorke appeared, in a state of overwhelming excitement, and, nothing doubting, straightway fell upon the new arrivals with an attempt to take the whole quintette into her ample embrace. No need of proofs for her; and, seeing this, the captain's doubts were dispersed, and he began a vigorous hand-shaking with each and every one of those present, including Brayton and myself, and repeating the process, until Brayton and I, feeling ourselves to be intruders in the midst of this family scene, made good our escape. Not, however, before 'Matildy Jane' had appeared, with tone, look, and manner, which you who know 'Matildy Jane' do not need to have described, denouncing the woman and children as 'ampostors,' and bidding them begone."

"And you do not think that the woman is a fraud?" asked aunt Emily.

"I do not, Mrs. Rutherford; and neither did

Brayton," answered Fred Winston. "And, besides the letter and marriage certificate which were in her possession, making good her pretensions, she had an honest face, and appeared respectable, — far too much so for the wife of such a scallywag as old Yorke's son is said to have been."

"If the Yorkes allow her claim, and take in this numerous family, it will interfere with your plans for Mrs. Yorke, uncle," I said.

"Not at all," said uncle Rutherford, who, when he had once made up his mind to a thing, would move heaven and earth to carry it out, and who often insisted upon benefiting people against their will. "Not at all. The new family can be left here to keep Matilda Jane company while her father and mother are away. There is all the more reason now that Mrs. Yorke should be cured of her lameness; and I believe that it can be done."

Blessed with the most sanguine of dispositions, as well as with the kindest and most generous of hearts, he always believed, until it was proved otherwise, that the thing he wished could be done.

"Milly," said aunt Emily, suddenly turning to my sister, "will you come down to the Yorkes' with me?"

Milly assented readily; and the two kindred spirits set forth together.

"The blessed creatures!" said Fred Winston. "What unlimited possibilities the arrival of this infirmary opens up to them. I knew that they would be off at once to inquire into the condition of the sick and wounded."

"And to find out how many candidates there may be for the hospital cottage and other refuges," I added.

But the two good Samaritans, as they afterwards reported, were not so appalled by the state of things at the Yorkes' cottage, as Mr. Winston's tale had prepared them to be. Perhaps matters had improved since he had left two hours since, or the stricken family had at once accommodated themselves to the change in their circumstances. Certain it is that aunt Emily and Milly found peace and serenity reigning: Mrs. Yorke with the little cripple in her capacious lap, coddling and petting her as the good soul well knew how to do; the captain piloting the blind child about the house and garden, familiarizing him with different objects, by which he might learn his own way about by his acute sense of touch; the youngest — a teething, not consumptive, baby — fast asleep; and even the recalcitrant "Matildy Jane" tolerably pleasant and good-natured beneath the fascinations of a handsome, sturdy urchin four years old, who, undaunted by her hard face and snappish voice, insisted upon following her around, and "helping" her in her manifold occupations. He

was a boy who did not know how to be snubbed,
and had fairly won his way with his ungracious
aunt, by sheer persistence in his unwelcome attentions. To all her hospitable intimations that he
and his family had brought an immense addition
to her cares and labors, — which certainly was
true, — he opposed smiles and caresses, and as-
surances that so long as he was there he would
share and lighten all these; appearing to think
that she complained and scolded only to draw
forth his sympathy and aid.

Who could stand out against such a fellow?
Not even "Matildy Jane." And she had succumbed; at least, so far as he was concerned.

The mother of the helpless group, pale, feeble,
and careworn though she was, had already shown
herself eager to lessen, so far as possible, the
burden she had brought upon the family of her
husband, and sat peeling potatoes from a huge
basket on the one side, while a pan of apples, duly
pared and quartered, stood awaiting the oven
upon the other. Plainly Matilda Jane had had no
scruples of delicacy in availing herself of the
services of her newly arrived sister-in-law.

"What *are* you going to do with them all,
Captain Yorke?" asked Milly, pityingly, as she
stood beside the old sailor in the porch, while
aunt Emily interviewed Mrs. Yorke and the
widow. "This is such a care for you."

"Do with 'em?" repeated the veteran, apparently quite undismayed by the prospect before him. "Waal, I reckon we've got to be eyes an' backs an' lungs to 'em, for they've run mighty short of them conveniences. Let alone Theodore, an' that feller over there," — nodding towards the kitchen-door, within which Matilda Jane was to be seen mixing biscuit, with the boy beside her, his round, fat arms up to the elbows in the dough, with which he was bedaubing himself and every thing about him, unrestrained by his subdued aunt, — "let alone that feller over there, there ain't the makin' of a hull one among 'em. I guess they've got to be took care of ; an', if the Almighty hadn't a meant us to do it, he wouldn't a sent 'em here. Them's my opinions, an' me an' Mis' Yorke we ain't the ones to throw back his orderin's an' purposin's in his face. They do seem a bit like a hospital full, though, don't they ? " he added, unconsciously expressing Mr. Winston's view of the situation. " Me an' Mis' Yorke, we foun' out the truth of the Scriptur' sayin', how sharper than an achin' tooth it is to have a thankless child, an' Tom, — I don't min' sayin' it to you, — he *was* thankless enough, though he's dead an' gone, an' his old father ain't the one to cast stones at him now. But me an' Mis' Yorke, we don't want to make out the truth of that other Scriptur', that the sins of the father shall be visited on the children, — leastways, not Tom's children ; they ain't to blame for his short-comin's ; an', meanin' no disrespec' nor onbelief, *that* Scriptur' do always seem to me a little hard on the children. Maybe — who knows — them youngsters will ha' brought a blessin' with 'em ; an' my opinions is they has, when I see Mis' Yorke a cuddlin' an' croonin' over that little hunchback. Now she's awful contented an' easy-minded like to have somethin' to pet, for she's allers a hankerin' after babies an' them sort of critters. We was kinder took aback, for sartain, when Maria, — her name's Maria, Tom's widder's is, — when she come right in with the hull crowd followin', an' John Waters' wagon, what they come from the station in, standin' at the gate, an' all the luggage in it ; an' them gentlemen was here gettin' bait an' askin' about the fishin', an' Matildy Jane she kinder flew out, an' one of the little ones was hollerin', — an' it was all kinder Bedlamy. But it's all come right now ; an' Maria, she's a willin' soul, an' if Jabez," the old man's son-in-law, and a power in the household, "if Jabez an' Charlotte don't be grumpy over it, we'll all get along as pretty as a psalm-book. Jabez, he an' Charlotte has gone to Millville for the day, an' all this is unbeknownst to them."

Clearly, the captain was somewhat in dread of Jabez and Jabez's opinions ; but Milly had no fear that the strangers would be sent adrift in deference to these.

But something must be done to help the old people with the burden which had so suddenly fallen upon them. The gray-haired seaman was comparatively vigorous still, but his sea-faring days were over; and while he had put by a sum sufficient to keep him, his good wife, and "Matildy Jane" in comfort, this unlooked for addition to the family, helpless and crippled as the grandchildren were, would be too great a drain upon his little fund. As this had been placed in father's hands for investment, we knew to a fraction what he had to depend upon, and that it was not enough to provide for all. The sturdy independence of the captain would no doubt revolt against the idea of receiving any actual pecuniary assistance, as would that of his wife; but some way must be contrived of lessening their responsibilities and cares. Jabez Strong and his wife must share these, although he might and probably would be "grumpy;" but even then it would be hard to meet all demands, without depriving the old couple of their accustomed comforts. The cheerful, it-will-all-come-right spirit in which they had received the intruders, — *I* could not look upon them in any other light, — made us all the more anxious to do this; and, before night, Milly and I were exercising our brains with all manner of expedients for accomplishing it without hurting their pride and their feelings.

Meanwhile, our elders, with less of enthusiasm perhaps, but in a more practical spirit, were considering the same matter; and the little ones, our

Allie and Daisy, having also heard of the influx of children at the Yorkes' cottage, had laden themselves with toys and picture-books, and persuaded mammy to escort them thither. Our little sisters had so burdened themselves, that they needed assistance to transport all these gifts to Captain Yorke's house; and they could not look for any great amount of this from mammy, who had all she could do to convey her own portly person, and the enormous umbrella without which she never stirred, as a possibly needed protection against sun or rain, as the case might be. So they begged that Bill and Jim might act as carriers, coaxing Thomas to spare them from pantry duty,— a matter not attended with much difficulty, as the old butler was only too willing to indulge them on all occasions, even to the length of taking double work on his own shoulders.

They all set forth on their errand of charity in high glee; but Jim returned from the expedition with a face and air of such portentous gravity, so different from his usual happy-go-lucky bearing, that Milly was moved to ask if any thing unpleasant had occurred.

"Captain Yorke nor his folks didn't do nothin', Miss Milly," answered Jim.

"Who, then?" asked Milly.

"Well, no *one*, Miss Milly," he replied. "I was on'y thinkin' what a lot of 'em there was, an' it bothers me."

"So many Yorkes, do you mean?" queried Milly, rather wondering at his evident perturbation.

"Such a many blind an' hunchback an' sick folks," he said; "an' how are they all goin' to be done for. The more you try to do for some of 'em, the more of 'em seem to come up. There's Matty and Tony Blair, who me an Bill has took into our keepin' soon as we get to the city; an' now here comes a Yorke hunchback, an' a Yorke blind, an' a Yorke sick baby, all sudden like; an' I say that's pretty hard on the ole captain. I like the captain firstrate, I do, Miss Milly; an' I don't like to see him put upon that way. Some of us ought to see to 'em for him, but you can't do for all."

"No, Jim," Milly said, soothingly, to the young philanthropist, "we cannot do for all who need; but, if each one does his or her mite, we can among us greatly lighten the load of human suffering; and that is what we must all try to do, without making ourselves unhappy over that which is beyond our reach or means."

"*You* did a mighty big mite, when you did for Bill an' me, Miss Milly," said her pupil and *protégé*, looking gratefully at her. "There ain't no halfway 'bout you, Miss Milly. But I would like to help Captain Yorke, if I could; an' I was thinkin', could I do up them sums again 'bout the peanuts, an' get out a share for the Yorkes."

Milly laughed, for she had heard of Jim's plans, and of the various objects which were to be benefited by the "peanut-undertaking;" and, as frequent new claims and claimants appeared to share in the profits, she argued that the proportion of each would be small.

"Jim," she said, "I think I would not undertake to help the Yorkes as well as all the other people you have upon your list. They shall not be allowed to suffer, you may be sure; Mr. Rutherford and Mr. Livingstone will see to that."

"Miss Milly," he answered, reproachfully, "I on'y didn't reckon up Captain Yorke an' his folks before, 'cause they hadn't need of it. Now they will, with all that raft of broke-up children on 'em; an' do you think I'd go to passin' 'em over when they was so good to me? No, that I wouldn't; I ain't never goin' to forget how Mis' Yorke nussed me, an' made much of me, when I was sick there in her house; an' they were good to me, too, when I was a little chap, an' got shipwrecked on to the shore. Miss Milly, do you know," — hesitatingly, — "I'd liever take some out of the 'lection expenses share, than to pass over the Yorkes. I would, really, Miss Milly."

Truly, our Milly was reaping a rich fruit of generosity, loyalty, and earnest endeavor, from the seed of self-sacrifice and charity which she herself had shown in faith and hope. And this, too, in ground which the on-lookers had judged to be so hardened and stony that no harvest was to be gathered therefrom. Oh, my Milly, sweet soul,

> "Great feelings hath she of her own,
>   Which lesser souls may never know."

CHAPTER IV.

"FOOD FOR THE GODS."

CHAPTER IV.

"FOOD FOR THE GODS."

BEHOLD our household now settled in our city
home, — our summer by the sea, with all its many
pleasures, and its measure of perplexities and anx-
ieties, a thing of the past; our stay at Oaklands,
where papa had enjoyed himself to his heart's
content, all the more for his enforced absence of
the previous months, also over; and the different
members of the family, according to his or her
individual taste, occupied with divers plans and
projects for the winter's duties and diversions.

In view of certain contingencies which were
likely to arise in the future, — father and mother
said in the *far* future; and, indeed, although it was
pleasant to contemplate them from a distant
standpoint, I was in no haste to leave my dearly
beloved home, — in view of these, and with the
comfort and well-being of a certain young man
before my eyes, to say nothing of my own pride
in my housekeeping capabilities, I had chosen to
enlist myself as a member of a "cooking-class."
Said cooking-class was to meet once a week, in
the afternoon, at the house of each member, in

turn, when we were to try our maiden hands on the composition of any such dishes as we might choose; after which, certain martyrs — namely, the aforesaid young man, and sundry of his friends and associates — were to be allowed to join us, and, in case they were not too fearful of consequences, to test the results of our efforts. Milly, who had a regular engagement for the afternoon appointed, was not able to aid in the culinary efforts, but pleaded, that, as she contributed a sister, she might be allowed to join the later entertainment of the evening. And the plea was considered all sufficient, for who would not choose Milly when she might be had? So said Bessie Sandford, our inseparable friend and intimate; and there was no dissenting voice among the gay circle of girls.

She did not intend, however, to be without her share in the flesh-pots which were to furnish the more substantial part of the entertainment; and having a natural gift for cooking, — a faculty in which I was altogether wanting, — she promised to prepare some dainty dish beforehand, and send it as her share in the feast.

My last essay in that line had been in the shape of some gingerbread, of which article of diet father was very fond, and I had exerted my energies on his behalf. When it was presented at the Sunday-evening tea-table, the family, excepting papa, contented themselves with viewing it respectfully from a distance ; even old Thomas, as he passed the plate, regarding it doubtfully and askance.

Father heroically endeavored to taste it ; but mother, whose regard for his physical well-being outweighed even her consideration for my feelings, protested ; and, with an air of relief, he obeyed the suggestion.

"What did you say it is ? Ginger *bricks ?*" asked Douglas.

I took no notice of this, but later bade Thomas take all the gingerbread down-stairs.

"Yes, Miss," he answered, with an "I wouldn't care if I were you" sort of an air; and the gingerbread disappeared. The next morning, however, as I went to the store-room to execute some small order for mother, our old cook confronted me.

"Miss Amy," she said, "whatever will I do with that gingerbread? There isn't one in the kitchen will touch it, not even them b'ys; an' all's mostly grist that comes to their mills."

"Oh, give it away to any one that comes," I answered indifferently, and concealing, as I best might, my chagrin at this added mortification.

But later in the day, Allie and Daisy, returning from their walk with mammy, rushed into the house in a state of frantic indignation.

"Amy, Amy," they cried; "Mary Jane gave your gingerbread to a tramp, and he looked at it and smelled it and tasted it, and then just laid it on the area steps and ran away. And Jim saw him; and he picked up the gingerbread, and broke it by throwing it on the sidewalk, and then threw the pieces at the tramp; and one hit him, and it was so hard it seemed to hurt him, but he just ran all the faster."

From that time, more than a year since, I had forsworn all manner of cooking, but now it seemed to me that the exigencies of the case required me to turn my thoughts to the matter; hence, when it was proposed, I had been only too ready to join the cooking-class.

The lady who had, from pure love of her kind, and a special interest in young girls, undertaken to superintend and direct our efforts, was an old friend of my mother and aunt Emily; the dearest, the sweetest, the most guileless, of maiden ladies, with a simplicity and lack of worldly knowledge which were almost childlike, but very talented, and with a mind intelligent and cultivated to an unusual degree.

She was also famous among us for all kinds of handiwork, — for the delicious cakes, soups, and all manner of dishes which she could concoct; for her painting and drawing, and her exquisite and original fancy-work. Simple, although delicate, in her tastes, her personal wants were but few; and being possessed of a small income, which placed her beyond the need of employing her varied talents on her own behalf, she delighted in turning them to account for others. She stood singularly alone, with no direct family ties or responsibilities; and probably no human being but herself ever knew the amount of work accomplished by those slender, high-bred looking hands for the benefit and delight of others. The beautiful paintings and embroideries which she sent to the various societies for art work, and which were always accepted without demur, meeting as they did with an ever ready sale, brought their profits, not to her, but to others less gifted and more needy than herself. And many a dainty trifle wrought by her graced some sick-room, or home of straitened means, where there was neither time nor talent to be given for such adornment.

Careless as to the prevailing mode, although exceedingly neat about her own personal attire, she was somewhat quaint and old-fashioned in appearance; at least, she had been until a short time since, when Milly and I, with Bessie Sandford, who was also a distant relation of Miss Craven's, had taken her in hand, and by dint of a little teasing, and much persistence and coaxing, had induced her to submit herself to our dictation in the matter of dress. But she could not, quite yet, reconcile herself to our requirements; at least, not without a little flutter and protest against such innovations as we insisted upon, — against tied-back skirts, hair a little more in the fashion than she had been accustomed to wear hers, and collars and fichus of a more modern date:

Hearing, the dear soul, that certain of our circle of girls were anxious to attain some practical knowledge of cooking, and to attach to the acquisition of that knowledge such "fun" as we might, she had offered, when applied to for certain of her receipts, to instruct the class which we were desirous of forming. The offer was eagerly seized upon, and so it came to pass that she had been installed as teacher and director of the mysteries in which we were about to dabble.

Miss Craven, — "cousin Serena," as we always called her — had been one of the warmest advocates of Milly's cause, when that young woman was intent on taking upon herself the charge of Bill and Jim ; and, had Milly not been allowed to do so, I think that she would have undertaken it herself. She was continually making little gifts to these boys, not always, it is true, just adapted to their needs or to their fancies ; but they had the grace, rough as their antecedents had been, to appreciate the kindness which prompted them ; and their room in the stable was decked with many a little bit of ornamentation bestowed by her. For one of her pet theories was, that one could educate the masses to a refining love of art, if one only kept such elevating influences constantly before them.

The first meeting of the cooking-class was held

at our house. Most of the girls were content to try their hands on this occasion on some simple dish; but I — more ambitious, and also for excellent reasons of my own — had determined to provide a certain delicate and highly flavored cream. In order that there might be no failure in this, and that I might, by an unqualified success, retrieve my reputation, I surreptitiously sought in advance two or three private lessons from Miss Craven. These she was only too ready to give; and after practising at home, closely following her directions, and assisted by old Thomas, who was almost as anxious for my triumph as I was myself, I succeeded in turning out my cream, pure, rich, white, just the right consistency, and deliciously flavored. It was but a small quantity, however; just a trial sample, not enough for family distribution; and, calling Allie and Daisy to the secret session which Thomas and I were holding in the butler's pantry, I divided the luscious morsel between them, exacting, first, the most solemn promise of secrecy. Allie demurred to this at first, having conscientious scruples about keeping any thing from mother; but she was finally persuaded to look upon it as a preparation for an agreeable surprise, as I assured her that this was only the prelude to a more extensive treat to the whole family, as well as the class. Moreover, the sight of the dainty, and Daisy's enjoyment of it, were too much for her, she having rather a leaning towards the flesh-pots.

I was quite uplifted in my own estimation for the next twenty-four hours or so, and pleased myself mightily with the thought of out-doing all the other girls with my dainty, luscious dish. Allie and Daisy could be trusted "not to tell," when they had once given their promise; but they went about with a portentous aspect of having a secret, which almost made me regret that I had taken them into my confidence.

It being leap-year, and our advantages, or possibly disadvantages, in connection with that period being about to come to an end with the close of the year, we had determined upon making the most of them. Hence our guests, when they should arrive, were to submit to be waited upon, and to receive such attentions as they were accustomed to bestow upon us.

The day and the hour had arrived, and the members of the class, each one with an enormous protecting apron over her pretty dress, had assembled in our front basement, which, being convenient to the kitchen and store-room, had been chosen as the workshop for the occasion. Each was intent on her own dish, and each in her turn was superintended and overlooked by cousin Serena; but merry talk and laughter held their own, in spite of business.

"What are you making, Amy?" asked Mollie Morgan. "How delicious and creamy that looks, and how readily you go to work about it. Why, I thought you were no cook at all; but one would think you had been doing that all your life. What is it?" she repeated, as I cast a guilty, deprecating look at Miss Craven. But cousin Serena had no thought of betraying me, and, although she must have heard, paid no attention to Mollie's remarks.

"It's food for the gods," I answered carelessly, as I tossed the luscious compound about with a spoon.

"Do you mean that is the name, or that it is your opinion that it is worthy to be food for the gods?" asked Bessie Sanford, who paused at my elbow, bearing in her hands a tray of delicate sponge-cakes.

"Both," I answered.

"Amy is ambitious; see what she is making, girls," said Mollie; and several, gathering round, peered at the diet of the gods with, as I imagined, envy and admiration.

"There!" I said, triumphantly, and as though I were a *cordon bleu*, accustomed to turn off feasts for an emperor — "There, now it is ready to go into the moulds. Oh, no, I have forgotten the flavoring. Jim," for the boy was there to wait upon us, and to run upon errands — "Jim, go and ask Mary Jane for a bottle of vanilla flavoring."

Now, I might have known better than to send Jim on this errand, for between him and Mary Jane there was a state of warfare, due, I must say, to her ill-temper and prejudice. Formerly it had been productive of much annoyance and discomfort to the household, and had at last reached such a climax, that father, who never interfered in domestic details, had unexpectedly taken the matter in hand, and given the old woman such a warning, that she had not since that time dared to give open vent to her dislike. But the fires, though smouldering, still were alive; and Jim never cared to ask her for any thing, or to carry a message to her.

However, now he ran into the kitchen, and presently returned with a bottle which he handed to me. Glancing at it, I saw that it was properly labelled, and I flavored with the contents according to directions; and, nothing doubting, then called upon cousin Serena to stamp it with her approbation, which she did. After which I poured the mixture into the moulds, and set it away.

Fairly well satisfied with the results of our afternoon's work, we removed such traces of it as had left their impress, took a short rest, and were ready in due time to receive our leap-year guests.

We were to have a high tea; the rest of our family, with cousin Serena, dining at an earlier hour than usual to accommodate us, and taking their later repast in the library.

There was naturally much fun and jollity over the reversal of the usual order of things, and we carried out our programme to the farthest; while our gentlemen displayed a degree of inefficiency and helplessness which would have disgraced a six-year-old girl with a moderate amount of sense.

All went well during the earlier part of the feast. Dish after dish was partaken of, and commended; and there was a universal chorus of approval for the fair cooks.

" It is going to pass off without a failure," I said to myself, recalling triumphantly the scepticism as to our capabilities, which some of our friends had testified.

And now appeared, in its turn, my own dish,— the "food for the gods,"— brought by Thomas and his assistants, with a little extra flourish as the work of their own young lady.

We were in groups of four, at little tables placed about the room ; and the gentlemen, as had been arranged, were helped first to each course. Happening to raise my eyes to address the youth upon my right hand, I saw his countenance suddenly distorted by a contortion expressive of any thing but pleasure. Turning involuntarily to my left-hand neighbor, who happened to be Mr. Winston, I saw a grimace, almost similar, pass over his face, followed by a look of blank astonishment at me.

Then came the voice of my brother Edward from an adjoining table, as he sat with uplifted spoon, gazing down upon the contents of his plate.

"Amy," he said, "what under the heavens is this?"

"Food for the gods," I answered, startled and dismayed; for I could not help seeing that something must be very wrong to betray Edward into such a breach of etiquette.

"Then we will not deprive the gods of it," said my brother; "and may the celestial — or was it for the infernal deities that it was compounded? — forgive you for inflicting this upon them. Winston, spare yourself, my dear fellow; the utmost stretch of politeness could not demand such a sacrifice of you."

For Fred Winston, true gentleman and loyal knight that he was, was making the most heroic efforts to swallow a little more of my handiwork.

And this from Edward, usually the most chivalrous of brothers!

I glanced around the room, and saw a similar state of affairs on every side. All those who had been unfortunate enough to taste the "food for the gods" wore a more or less distressed expression. I plunged my own spoon into my plate, and carried it to my mouth.

Pah! Any thing more nauseous I had seldom tasted. The gods were indeed to be pitied!

I covered my face with my hands as a laugh pealed around the room; and Norman came dashing into it, and up to me.

"Amy," he said, in a loud whisper which could

be heard by all, "mother says don't let any one touch that stuff of yours.   It's awful!"

"Awful" indeed!   But it was too late; enough tasting had been done to cover me, as I felt, with everlasting disgrace.

"Amy was so awfully cock-a-hoop about her new dish, too," began Norman; "and now"—

But his brotherly remarks were cut short by my left-hand neighbor, with an intimation, that, if he had any regard for his physical or mental well-being, he would at least postpone them.

Overcome with mortification and chagrin, I would fain have left the room, not only to hide my diminished head, but also to consult cousin Serena on the possible cause of this mishap, when Jim came up to me, and said, in an aside even louder than Norman's,—

"Miss Amy, it wouldn't poison none of 'em, would it?"

When Jim had any thing on his mind it must come out, regardless of time or place; and there was that in the boy's tone and manner which instantly convinced me that he knew more than appeared on the surface, and I turned hastily to him:—

"Poison any one?   Why should it?" I asked.

"It's the liniment, Miss Amy," he answered nervously; "an', if they was poisoned, me or you might be took up.   We'd best have a doctor, maybe."

Matters were growing serious; and springing from my seat, without apology to my guests, I bade the boy come into Thomas's pantry. Thither I was followed by Fred and Edward, who heard the confession of the frightened lad.

"It's the liniment, Miss Amy," he repeated. "Mary Jane's liniment for her rheumatics; but I think it ought to be her to be took up more than you an' me."

"Speak out, boy, and tell us what you mean," said Edward, imperatively; for he felt, that, if there was any reason for Jim's alarm, there was no time to be lost.

Thus pressed, Jim said that when I had sent him for the flavoring, he had caught up a bottle which he supposed to be the right one, and ran back without consulting the old cook.

Nothing doubting, I had made use of the contents; and he had possessed his soul in peace until a few minutes since, when Thomas had sent him on an errand to the kitchen, and he had heard Mary Jane bewailing the loss of her bottle of "rheumatiz liniment." She at once charged him with hiding it to torment her, but, before he could defend himself, one of the other servants asked what kind of a bottle it was; to which she replied, that it was a vanilla-bottle into which she had emptied the liniment, as that in which the lotion belonged had been cracked, and that she had stood it "just there."

A horrible conviction rushed upon Jim: "just there" was the place from which he had taken the bottle he brought to me. He dashed into the front basement, found there the bottle in question, and speedily verified his own fears ; then hurried up-stairs to prevent Thomas from taking in the "food for the gods." Alas! it was too late : the dish was already dispensed, a due portion having also been sent in to the tea-table in the library; and my disgrace was an accomplished fact.

Dread of the after consequences now took possession of Jim, and this impelled him to an immediate disclosure of the mistake. Indeed, none of us were without our misgivings; and Edward, sending for the bottle, went with it at once to our family physician, who lived but a few doors from us.

Dr. Graham laughed heartily when he heard of the mishap, and told Edward that there was no cause for alarm ; as, although he would not advise unlimited indulgence in the lotion as a beverage, such harmful qualities as its ingredients possessed would be reduced to a minimum when mixed in the proportion Edward mentioned with the other articles of which the "food for the gods" was compounded.

So the matter became a joke to every one but me and the old cook, who received a severe reprimand for her carelessness in putting the liniment in an improper receptacle, and then leaving it in an improper place.

Thus ended my attempt at culinary distinction ;
a regard for the well-being of my friends and even
for their lives, inducing me to quit the field without further trial of my powers.

What a long tale about a foolish mistake, it may
be said ; but, as "great events from little causes
spring," the results of that mistake were vast and
far-reaching, and we had not yet heard the last of
the "food for the gods."

CHAPTER V.

THE "MORNING BUGLE."

CHAPTER V.

"Look at this disconsolate pair; melancholy has evidently marked them for her own," said Bessie Sanford, as she and I crossed the corner of the square, bound for an afternoon walk; aimless, except in the search for fresh air and exercise.

The "disconsolate pair" were my little sisters, Allie and Daisy, who now approached, trundling their dolls' perambulators in front of them, and followed by mammy, who came limping after, also wearing a most lugubrious expression; but whereas their distress was plainly mental, her's was physical, drawn forth by pain.

"Old mammy has an attack of her pet bunion," I said, "and I suppose that the children are, in consequence, debarred from their walk, and they have but just come out. Poor little things! What do you say, Bessie, to taking them with us? They would be enchanted."

"So should I. By all means let us take them," answered Bessie, who had a love for children and their company, only second to my own.

"O, sister Amy!" cried both the little ones,

dropping the perambulators, and rushing up to us as soon as their eyes fell upon us, "Mammy's bunion hurts so, she can't take us to walk, and it's such a lovely day, and we want to go Jim's peanut-stand."

And the ever ready tears rushed to the eyes of Allie, who was prone to weep upon slight provocation ; and even Daisy, who was more philosophical, though younger, looked heart-broken.

Sunshine speedily succeeded the showers, however, for my proposal that they should accompany us was received with rapture ; and, taking their dolls into their arms, they abandoned the perambulators to the care of mammy, who hobbled towards home with them. This bunion was mammy's choice grievance, and she doubtless suffered much from it ; but it was an article of the family faith, that, when for any reason she was disinclined to take her walks abroad with the children, the bunion sympathized with this reluctance, and crippled her to an unusual extent.

"And where do you want to go?" I asked of the beaming pair, who were now hanging, the one on Bessie's arm, the other on mine. "Bessie and I do not much care which way we go."

"Oh," said Daisy, ecstatically, "if you would only take us to Jim's peanut-stand! Mother said we might go, and then mammy couldn't take us."

"It's not fash'nable, but it's very respectable, Amy," said Allie, impressively.

"But we cannot go to a peanut-stand, even though it belongs to Jim," I expostulated.

"But it's not in the street; it's — you know Johnny, the flower-man, sister?" said Allie.

"Johnny the flower-man" was a German florist on a small scale, who had a little glass-enclosed stand on the corner of the avenue next to that on which we lived, and who was extensively patronized by our family and many of our neighbors. His box of a place, cosey, warm, and fragrant, was a favorite resort of our children; and much of their pocket-money went to the purchase of the potted plants and cut flowers which he sold to them at a wonderfully reasonable rate. But what had the little German to do with Jim and his peanut-stand? Allie soon enlightened us.

"Jim was going to have the stand on that corner," she said, "and he had leave to do it; but mamma and aunt Emily said it would not do for Tony and Matty to sit out of doors in the cold weather; it would kill Matty, they said. And Jim was so disappointed, and he didn't know what to do; and one day when sister Milly sent him to Johnny's, he told him about it, and about Tony and Matty; and that lovely old Johnny, — Daisy and I ask God to bless him every night when we've done our own people, — he told Jim he could have a little corner of his store where it was all glass, and the stand could be seen from the street; and then Matty could sit there, and people would come in and buy her peanuts. Wasn't it good in him? We love Johnny, if he does squint, and smell of tobacco, and can't talk very plain."

"And then," said Daisy, taking up the tale in her turn, as Allie paused for breath, "and then there wasn't room there for the roaster, 'cause it's pretty squeezed up in Matty's corner, and in Johnny's store, too, wif the stand there; so Johnny's wife, who lives just a little bit of a way off, lets Tony have the roaster up in her room, and roast the peanuts, and then he runs very quick wif 'em over to Matty, or, if it's a nice, pleasant day, he has it put outside the door. But the smell of the peanuts gets mixed up wif the smell of the flowers, and that isn't so very nice."

"But Jim is making lots of money, he says," continued Allie; "'cause most always when people come in to buy flowers, Johnny tells 'em they'd better buy peanuts, too; and Jim printed a sign in German about peanuts inside, and put the meaning in English beneath, and he says he thinks he is doing a better business than if Matty sat outside. Norman and Douglas buy lots, but," with a little sigh, "mother don't like Daisy and me to eat peanuts. It would be a good way to do charity if she would let us; but sometimes we buy some, and give them to the servants."

Jim and his "peanut undertakin'," as Captain Yorke had called it, had, in the press of other and greater interests, almost passed from my mind, and I had made no inquiries about it lately ; but, as visions of numerous peanut-shells in the most unheard of places returned to my recollection, I could not doubt the truth of Allie's assertion in regard to my brothers.

While the children had been talking, we had been gradually walking on towards the desired haven, — the corner where the German florist had his tiny store ; and presently we came to it. The little glass enclosure was one mass of vivid green, and brilliant, glowing color ; for Johnny was remarkably successful in the treatment of his plants, and they always wore a thrifty, healthy aspect, delightful to behold.

Without, just at the side of the door of entrance, hung the sign described by Allie ; and Daisy at once drew our attention to it.

The "German" legend ran thus : —

> "Goot rost benuts ish incite, nein sents a quoort.
> Shtep in unt py."

The English translation followed : —

> "Good roost peanuts is inside, nine cents a quart.
> Step in and by."

Bessie and I were inwardly amused, but did not let it appear to the admiring children. Allie, however, had her own misgivings as to the absolute correctness of the sign, and said, doubtfully, —

"I suppose the German must be all right, because Jim says that is the way Johnny talks; but the English is not spelled quite right, is it, sister Amy?"

"Not altogether," I answered; "but perhaps it attracts more attention than it would do if it were quite correct, Allie, and that, you know, is the object of a sign or notice."

"Yees," said Allie, doubtfully, lingering behind a moment to scan the sign as I opened the door, and still inclined to criticise; "ye-es, but somebody might laugh if it is not spelled quite right."

"That is of no consequence so long as it does not hurt business," I said, shamelessly indifferent to the orthographical merits of the case. "Come in, Allie, we must not keep the door open too long."

At the farthest end of the crowded little cubby-hole, — all the more crowded, of course, for the accommodation which the good-hearted German had afforded to Jim's beneficiaries, — sat the little deformed Matty, behind her stand, on which were displayed a tempting pile of freshly roasted peanuts, and various bright, new measures. Outside, on the street, could be seen Tony, grinding away at his revolving roaster; for the day was so exceptionally lovely, that there could be nothing in the air to injure him, and he doubtless preferred its freshness, and the brilliant sunshine, to the presumably dark and stuffy quarters of Mrs. Johnny.

"AT THE FARTHEST END SAT THE LITTLE, DEFORMED MATTY.—*Page 96.*

Poor, poor Matty! Deformed, shrunken, and wizened, she was a painful contrast to all the beauty and brightness surrounding her in the little conservatory. Beyond the sympathy unavoidably drawn forth by her helpless and crippled condition, there was absolutely nothing to attract one toward her. She looked peevish and fretful, too, so far as there was any expression in the dull, heavy face. Was it to be wondered at? There had been but little of brightness in her young life; and as I looked from her to my little sisters, our petted household darlings, carefully guarded and shielded, so full of life and joyousness, so free from all pain or care, my heart swelled with thankfulness, that to them had been allotted no such fate, and with the desire to brighten the lot of this little unfortunate.

It was not so with her brother Tony: he was the jolliest, most active little cripple that ever hobbled round on one leg and a crutch. The celerity of his movements was something surprising; his voice was merry and cheery; and his ugly young face, despite the many hardships of his lot, generally wore a smile.

Now and then he would be seen with his face pressed against the glass, with a nod of good-fellowship to his sister or Johnny, or staring at such customers as happened to be within; and, if these proved to be Matty's patrons, he would watch the progress of the sale with great interest.

Then he would turn to his roaster, and work it violently for a few moments, then be off to the curbstone or crossing, exchanging some, probably not very choice, joke with some other street-gamin, or the conductor or driver of a passing street-car.

The children, Allie and Daisy, made their investments while I was taking these observations, and Bessie was purchasing cut-flowers from the old German. She was a good German scholar, and delighted the heart of the old man with the familiar language of the fatherland, which flowed glibly from her tongue. The consequence was, that that politic young woman left the florist's with three times the amount of flowers that I had, although I had spent just twice as much money. But, then, I could not speak German.

"I am going to take my flowers to cousin Serena," I said, after we had left the florist's, and exchanged a word or two with jolly little Tony as we passed. "Will you come and see her, Bessie?"

Bessie assented, and the two little ones were only too glad to accompany us. A visit to cousin Serena was always a treat to them.

"And we will give her the peanuts we bought; she likes peanuts," said Daisy, who, as well as Allie, had maintained a silence, quite unusual with them, during several minutes.

"But we'd like her and all our people to understand," said Allie, loftily, "that we buy peanuts because of Jim, and not at all because of Matty. She's the most unchristianest child we ever saw; and I think her soul is hunchback, too, just as well as herself."

I had seen that Matty had repelled the advances of the children, who had wished to show her their dolls, and to be kind to her; and I endeavored to soothe them, and excuse her, by telling them how much she had to suffer, and how her disposition might have been spoiled by all that she had undergone.

But my words made no impression; the children were not to be mollified. Allie still wore an air of outraged and offended dignity; and Daisy not only maintained that solemn silence, but she looked grieved and hurt. Our little ones were not accustomed to be snubbed, and took it hard when such an experience did befall them; but there was a preternatural gravity about them now, which excited my wonder.

"Why, Daisy," exclaimed Bessie, suddenly, "what is the matter with your cheek? It is all red and scratched. What have you been doing to yourself?"

"She didn't do it to herself," said Allie, indignantly, and before Daisy could speak. "We didn't want to tell tales; but, sister Amy and cousin Bessie, I think you are not very *noticeable*, not to see Daisy's cheek before this. We are very much disappointed in you."

We apologized humbly, saying that Daisy's broad felt hat had prevented us from seeing the state of her cheek before this, and inquired more minutely into the cause thereof.

With some reluctance the children told, that, while Bessie and I had been making our purchases of flowers, they had, after buying their peanuts, tried to make themselves agreeable to Matty; but she had proved far from responsive, and would not even look at the beautiful dolls which they proffered for her admiration. Believing that shyness alone was the cause of this ungraciousness, and filled with pity for her condition, Daisy had at last raised Matty's arm and placed her doll within it, when the cripple suddenly turned upon her, and drew the nails of the disengaged hand viciously down poor little Daisy's soft cheek, while, with the other, she threw the doll from her. Fortunately, the doll was not hurt; but the insult to her cherished darling had grieved Daisy more deeply than did the injury to herself. She had heroically refrained from crying out, or making any complaint, lest Johnny should be moved to espouse her cause, and avenge it on Matty; but it had gone to her heart, and to Allie's as well, that, after such forbearance, neither Bessie nor I should have noticed her plight. However, we made up for it now by an outburst of indignation and resentment, especially violent on my part; whereupon, the sage Allie turned my own moral

lecture, so lately delivered, upon myself, recalling
my exhortations to the effect that we should be
patient and forgiving with one so sorely afflicted
as Matty Blair.

When we reached cousin Serena's, a little arnica
and some French bonbons healed Daisy's wounds,
both mental and physical; but when happiness
and peace were once more restored, and she was
seated upon Miss Craven's lap, with Allie beside
her, and the box of chocolates between them,
cousin Serena herself was discovered to be in
a state of no small flutter and excitement.

"My dears," she said, "have you seen the
'Morning Bugle' of to-day?"

"No," I said, emphatically. "Father would
not allow that paper to come into our house."

"Nor would my father," said Bessie.

"He says it is a scandalous sheet," I added.
"He would not have it if there were not another
newspaper in the city."

"Nor would I in my own house," said Miss
Craven; "but," apologetically, "when one is in
a boarding-house, my loves, you know one cannot
control other people."

"I should think not," said Bessie. "It would
be hard, indeed, if you were held responsible for
the morals, or the literary tastes, of Mrs. Dutton's
other boarders."

"But you dearest of Serenas," I said, "you
know you need not read the 'Morning Bugle'

because some of the other people in the house take it. O Serena, Serena," reproachfully, "I thought better things of you! That *you* should allow your mind and morals to be poisoned in that way!"

"My dear Amy! My dear children!" exclaimed the dear, matter-of-fact old lady, who never knew when she was being teased, which made it all the more delightful to tease her. "My dear loves, you do not think I read that scandalous sheet! Why, this morning I should have said that nothing would induce me to touch it; but when Mrs. Dutton came up with the paper in her hand, and said, 'Is not this meant for your friends?' what could I do? I had to take it, and read the paragraph; and, my dears, here it is. Oh, I have been so unhappy all day about it! What will your father and brother do? Mrs. Dutton let me cut this out, when she saw how I felt about it."

I took the scrap of paper which she handed to me; and the blood rushed to my heart, as I read an item with the following heading : —

"A MADISON-SQUARE SENSATION."

It was a garbled and scurrilous account of the late little incident at our house, implying, indeed openly asserting, that there had been a wholesale attempt at poisoning. Names were not given, not even the initials under which the reporters of such gossip often pretend to disguise publicity, and in a measure avoid responsibility; but, to the initiated, there could be no doubt that the paragraph referred to my unlucky cookery. Further particulars, it was said, would be given at a later date, although it was difficult to obtain information, as the parties concerned had endeavored to hush up the matter; and "money is a power in this community."

I turned faint and giddy as I read; while Bessie, who looked over my shoulder, burst into a tempest of indignant exclamation.

"Dear child! Don't turn so white, Amy, my dear; I am so sorry I showed it to you," cried Miss Craven, aghast at my alarm and agitation. "It is outrageous, scandalous; but it cannot hurt you: you see no names are given. But I shall never forgive myself, for I told Mrs. Dutton about the 'food for the gods'. She was interested, you know, when you were here with me learning to make it, and asked me how it turned out. But she is discretion itself; she would not say a word, nor let any one know — Oh! my dear child, what shall I do? What shall we all do?"

But the vivid imagination with which I was credited by my friends, and which not unseldom did cause me many a needless foreboding, was rampant now; and visions arose before me of disgrace to the family, if those dreadful newspaper people did, as they threatened, "give further particulars," and perhaps go to greater lengths, and even print

my name in their horrible sheet.   Should I ever be
able to hold up my head again?   I sat in dumb,
terrified astonishment.

But here, Bessie, with her practical common
sense, came to the front, and brought me back to
reason.

"So that is the way you meant to make such a
success of your 'food for the gods,' is it, you
fraud?" she said, putting her hands on my shoulders, and playfully shaking me, "coming here and
practising with cousin Serena, forsooth; and the
rest of us experimenting with our first efforts.
O Amy, Amy, I would not have believed it of you.
And the gods themselves turned against you.
Their mills did grind exceeding sure that time,
and not so slowly, either; vengeance followed,
swift and sure.   You deserve this.   Cheating play
never prospers, Amy; and 'honesty is the best
policy,' and all that."

Meanwhile, the children were gazing from one
to another of their elders, not knowing what to
make of all this, — Allie uncertain whether or no
she had better call upon her ever ready tears,
Daisy bewildered, and at a loss to know upon
whom to bestow her sympathy, cousin Serena or
me; for I had not yet put my miserable imaginings
into words, and my startled looks alone appealed
to her; while Miss Craven was in a half-frantic
state of excitement; and, as for Bessie, she had
at first appeared furiously angry, and now, with a

sudden change, was turning the whole thing into a laugh. What could it all be about? wondered these innocents.

"Oh," I gasped at last, "what shall we do? What will papa say? What will uncle Rutherford say? What will Edward say? What will " —

"Yes, my dear, what will Fred say?" Bessie completed my unfinished sentence, as I paused, overwhelmed. "They will each and every man of them settle this matter, to the anguish of that editor, if I know them, and without one word of trouble or publicity to you, or any one of the family. You dear goose, you, to make such a personal matter of it. Why not, Jim; why not still more, Mary Jane?"

"I must go home," I said, feeling a burning desire to find at once my natural protectors, and to place the matter in their hands; and go I would and did, cousin Serena accompanying me, with Bessie and the children. We paused by the way, to knock at Mrs. Dutton's door, and to ask her if she had called the attention of any of the other boarders to that shameful paragraph.

Mrs. Dutton, motherly, gentle, refined, a lady in birth, education, and manner, and with a warm corner in her heart for the girls, big and little, who ran in and out on their visits to Miss Craven, assured us that she had not done so; and, in answer to my anxious inquiries, said, also, that she had never mentioned the incident of the " food for the gods " to any one.

It is not necessary to state, that my mankind were incensed when they saw the objectionable paragraph, although they did make light before me of my terrors and apprehensions ; and it remained a fact, that Edward went at once to a friend and brother lawyer, to request him to take steps to prevent any further annoyance or developments in the matter. It so happened, said this gentleman, that he had a hold upon the editor of the " Morning Bugle," which that personage would be very sorry to have him use to his disadvantage ; and he assured Edward that he would settle the affair in such a way that none of us need fear any future trouble or publicity.

How the thing had become known so as to afford matter for newspaper gossip, we could not tell, and did not much care to know ; probably, through the talk of the servants, who had, of course, been acquainted with all the particulars of the unfortunate incident. Exaggeration, and a wilful desire to falsify a trifle to the discredit of those concerned, had done the rest ; but our lawyer friend's remedy proved effectual, and the " Morning Bugle " was silenced.

CHAPTER VI.

UNCLE RUTHERFORD'S PRIZE.

CHAPTER VI.

UNCLE RUTHERFORD, the most generous, the most benevolent, of men, had, nevertheless, the most exasperating way of carrying out his kindnesses. He would suggest or hint at something delightful, and which just met the views or desires of his hearers, dwell upon it for a time, then, after leading one to the very height of expectation, would apparently put the matter entirely from his thoughts, and for days, weeks, or months, nothing further would be heard of it.

To urge its fulfilment, or to endeavor to discover what his intentions might be, was never productive of any good; on the contrary, his intimates believed that this still further deferred the wished-for result. Even aunt Emily, his much beloved and trusted wife, had learned to possess her soul in patience, when he was supposed to be revolving any thing of this nature in his mind.

The question of Jim's future had never been alluded to by him since that day last September, when it had been discussed at our seaside-home; and now it was nearly Christmas, and Milly was on tenter-hooks to know if there was any thing favorable in store for her *protégé.* She knew better, as I have said, than to hurry matters, or to ask any questions. That uncle Rutherford had not forgotten it, however, was evident from the way in which he watched, and apparently studied, the boy's ways and character; Jim all the while quite unconscious of such scrutiny.

"Milly," he said, on the evening of the day following that of the episode of the "Morning Bugle,"—"Milly, I see that boy Jim has a temper which needs some curbing."

Now, "a temper" was uncle Rutherford's *bête noir*, albeit his own was not of the most placid type, and that it was liable to be roused to what he called "just indignation," on that which to others appeared small provocation. The flash was always momentary, but it was severe while it lasted; and it had ever been a cross and a stumbling-block to him, spite of the polite name by which he called its manifestations. It was probably the recollection of the trouble it had brought to him, and of the struggles which even now it cost him, an elderly man, which made him so intolerant of its existence in others, especially the young. It is not necessary for the reader to quote the oft-repeated proverb about dwellers in glass houses, for uncle Rutherford was perfectly conscious of the exceeding fragility of his own panes; and his only wish was to warn and help those who were cursed with a fiery, impetuous spirit like his own.

That Jim was a victim to this, no one could deny, and Milly did not attempt to dispute it now; she merely assented meekly, and acknowledged that Thomas and Bill were constantly rescuing him from street-fights, and other escapades of that nature. And there were times when, in some of his rages with his fellow-servants, the raised tones of his furious voice had penetrated to the upper regions, and called for interference from the higher powers; but these occasions were becoming more and more rare. His devotion and loyalty to Milly and the other members of the family who had befriended him were not infrequently the occasion of these outbursts ; for, at the smallest real or fancied injury or slight to any one among us, he was up in arms, and his tongue and his fists were only too ready to avenge us. He was very impatient, too, of any allusion by others to his own origin, or to the state of degradation from which Milly had rescued him and Bill, although he would discuss it more or less freely with her, and with his boon companion and chum.

"What has Jim been doing now, uncle?" asked Milly; her hopes for the advancement of the boy through uncle Rutherford's means falling, as she wondered if he were noticing only to find out the flaws in a by no means faultless character.

"Just that; been in a street-fight, or what

would have proved a street-fight, if I had not come upon the scene just in time to call him to his senses, and to order him into the house instanter," said our uncle; "and, from what I could learn, he attacked a boy much larger than himself, on very small provocation,—merely, that the boy disputed his claim to the name of Livingstone, by which it appears he chooses to dub himself."

"He does not know his own name," said Milly, apologetically.

"That is no reason that he should call himself by yours," rejoined uncle Rutherford.

"It is something of the old feeling of feudal times, or that which used to make our Southern slaves adopt the surnames of their, masters, I think," said Edward. "Jim thinks that 'them as belongs to Livingstones ought to be called Livingstone.'"

"Captain Yorke proposed to him to take his," said I, "but Jim declined, on the ground that Yorke was not so nice a name as Livingstone for the 'President of these States.' He has it in his heart, too, to confer honor upon our family name by the reflected glories of the position to which he aspires."

"The boy's spirit of gratitude and appreciation, at least, are worthy of all credit," said aunt Emily.

"And, whatever he may owe to Milly and the family, he has already repaid the debt with interest," said mother; her thoughts, doubtless, recurring to Jim's heroic rescue of the youngling of her flock — her baby Daisy — from a frightful death; to say nothing of his sturdy fidelity to the welfare of our household and property under circumstances of great temptation and fear during the last summer.

"I had thought," said uncle Rutherford, slowly, and Milly's face lighted up; was it coming at last? "I had thought, if you judged well of it," turning to mother, "of having him go to the public grammar-school for this year, and there to test his capabilities, not only in the way of learning, but even more in his power and desire to control this temper of his. If he gives satisfaction, and proves himself worthy of it, let him continue at school until he is fitted for it, when I will give him a scholarship which I own in the School of Mines. At present it is filled, but will fall vacant about the time that Jim will be ready to take it. There is another boy on whom I have my eye, who has the same bent for a calling that Jim has, and whom I wish to befriend and help; but he, too, has faults which I hope to see him correct, — faults in some respects more serious than Jim's, —and the prize will lie between these two. Whoever proves himself most worthy and capable, the most steady, reliable, and best master of himself, shall take the scholarship. But, if Jim goes regularly to school, he will, of course, have to resign,

in a great measure, his duties as a household ser-
vant. Are you willing to have him do this? For
I do not wish or intend to inconvenience you.
What is your opinion of the whole matter?"

"Ask Milly," said mother, "she is the arbitress
of his fate."

And uncle Rutherford looked to that young
damsel.

"What say you, Milly?"

There was little need of words. Milly's sparkling eyes and flushed cheeks spoke for her. This
was so much beyond any thing she had hoped for
on behalf of the boy, that at first it seemed to her
almost too good to be true. And, yet, there were
lions in the way. And, after a moment's consideration, she answered, somewhat hesitatingly, —

"I hardly know what to say, sir."

We all looked in astonishment. Most of the
family thought that Milly's hopes and ideas for
the future of her *protégés* were rather quixotic
and unreasonable, aiming at taking them out of
their proper sphere. But here her clear judgment
and good sense saw some objections to uncle
Rutherford's plan.

"You are very kind, more than kind, uncle,"
she continued. "Such an offer is, indeed, a
'chance' for Jim such as I had never dreamed of,
and there could be no question between this, and
his training as a household servant; but I fear for
the effect of the emulation upon him. If he is to

gain this prize by outstripping or defeating another, the spirit of victory for victory's sake will take possession of 'him, and he will make every thing give way to it."

"Then he will not prove himself worthy of the prize," said uncle Rutherford, who had a fancy for inciting young people to efforts of this nature, and who was always holding out some prize to be striven for.

"I don't know," said Milly, a little wistfully; "he is so impulsive, so eager, so almost passionate, in the pursuit of any object on which he has set his mind, that I am afraid too much of the spirit of rivalry will enter into his efforts to win this."

"And," put in Norman, "he will be so cock-a-hoop if he is set to study for a scholarship, that there will be no bearing him, and " —

But Norman was brought to an abrupt silence, by a quick reprimand from father; while uncle Rutherford took no notice of the interruption, but continued to urge upon Milly the acceptance of his project. It undoubtedly presented so many advantages for Jim, that these finally outweighed her scruples, and she agreed thereto with earnest thanks.

"Who is the other fellow, uncle?" asked Norman the irrepressible, "any one whom we know?"

"Yorke's eldest grandson," said uncle Rutherford.

"That sneak!" ejaculated Norman.

"So that is your opinion of him," said uncle, turning towards Norman. "Well, I have not myself much confidence in the boy. There is something about him which I do not like; he is not frank and outspoken. He is a bright lad, however, ambitious, and disposed to make the most of any opportunities which fall in his way; and, for old Yorke's sake, I would like to help him. Yorke pinched and saved and denied himself, to give that boy's father an education, and illy he was repaid by the graceless scoundrel, who dissipated his father's hard-earned savings, and half broke his heart, and that of his poor mother. The captain is building on this boy's future, now; and, if he does not show himself fit for a college course, he may, at least, when he has had sufficient schooling, be taught a trade, and share the burden of the family support. We shall see which will win the prize, Jim or Theodore."

Douglas began to laugh in his quiet way, but Norman spoke out again.

"Won't there be jolly rows, when those two come to be pitted against one another," he said. "Either one will do his best to keep the other from winning it, even if he don't care for it himself."

There was too much reason to believe that Norman's prophecy would prove true. From the time that Theodore Yorke had appeared at his grandfather's, a pronounced state of antagonism had declared itself between the two boys ; and this had continued up to the time of our leaving the Point. Jim, who was a great favorite with the old captain and his wife, seemed to look upon Theodore as an interloper, and trespasser upon his preserves ; and the latter at once resented the familiar footing on which he found Jim established in his grandfather's house, although he himself had never been there before, and had hitherto been a stranger to all of his father's family.

It had required the exercise of the strictest authority to maintain any thing like a semblance of peace during the remainder of our stay at the seaside ; and there were occasional outbreaks, which tended to any thing but comfort to Captain Yorke's household. Our house and grounds were forbidden to Theodore Yorke, in consequence of this feud ; but Jim's duties called him, at times, to the home of the old sailor, whence he was accustomed to bring the daily supply of milk for the consumption of the family, and where he had been wont to linger as long as he dared when sent on this errand. More than once had he returned with a black eye, cut lip, or other adornment of a warlike nature ; and several milk-pails had been degraded from things of usefulness, by reason of being used as weapons of offence and defence.

And, although he knew all this, here was uncle Rutherford actually setting up these two already

belligerent lads as rivals in the race for learning
and character, with such a prize in the future to
the winner.   His object would defeat itself.   Was
it to be supposed that tempers would be controlled,
that any little tendency to take advantage of an
enemy would be smothered, under these circumstances ?

"Dear uncle," said Milly, whose face had fallen
when she heard who was to be the rival candidate,
"Jim is my charge; and you will not think me
ungracious, if I say that I cannot consent to let
him enter the lists against Theodore Yorke.   I
know only too well that it would arouse all his
bad passions.   As I said before, rivalry in any case
would not be best for him, but, against Theodore,
it would be simply ruinous ; and I would rather see
him remain under Thomas's tuition, learning to be
a thorough and efficient servant, and to control
his temper because right is right, than to have
him take the first honors in any college in the
world, if these are to be purchased by the fostering
of an envy and jealousy which I am sure would be
the result of your plan."

"Saint Millicent is right, as usual, when her
brands snatched from the burning are concerned,"
said father, putting his arm over her shoulder.
"I quite agree with her, Rutherford.   We shall
always see that both those boys, Jim and Bill, are
well provided for ; and neither of them shall lack
for such an amount of education as may fit him to

make his way in some respectable calling. To Jim we owe a debt which far outbalances the benefit he has received at our hands." And papa's eye turned, with lingering tenderness, to the far corner of the room, where Allie and Daisy, unconscious of the weighty matters which were being discussed among their elders, were absorbed in happy play with dolls and dog. "When he is old enough and steady enough, we will set him up in some line of business which he may choose — eh, Milly? — that is, if he shows any aptitude for a mercantile life; and he may work his way thence to the Chief Magistracy, if he find the path which he imagines lies open to him. As for Bill, he runs Wall Street, you know; and his voice, and talent for music, would make *his* way in the world. There is something that must be cultivated."

"Do you mean, Millicent, that you are actually going to refuse my offer for Jim?" said uncle Rutherford, in a tone of deep displeasure; for he did not like to be circumvented when he had set his mind upon a thing, especially if it chanced to be one of his philanthropic schemes. And that same quick temper, which he had found his own bane, showed itself now, in the flush which mounted to his brow, and the sudden flash which shot from his eyes. "Then, my dear, all I have to say is" —

That was all he had to say; and Milly escaped something which would have hurt her feelings, and which uncle Rutherford himself would have regretted when another moment should have passed, for aunt Emily laid her hand upon his arm, half-whispering, as a noted imperial wife was once wont to do to her impetuous and fiery lord, "Nicholas, Nicholas!" and with a like, calming effect, for further words were arrested on his lips.

There was a little awkward silence for a moment; then, as if by a sudden inspiration, uncle Rutherford said pleasantly, —

"How absurd we all are! What need for either boy to know that he is a rival to the other? Put the reward before each one, and tell him that the winning of it depends upon himself, and then we shall see."

So, then, was it settled, to the satisfaction of all; uncle Rutherford, it is true, a little disappointed that the stimulus of emulation was not to enter into the contest; and the discussion was here brought to a close by the appearance of Bill with a box of flowers "for Miss Amy."

But there was a factor in the case, upon which we had not counted.

In the privacy of their room over the stable, Bill and Jim held converse that night; and this was the substance of their communing, divested of unnecessary adornments of speech, with which those young gentlemen were wont to garnish their conversation when removed from the restraints of polite society.

"There's a big thing up for you, Jim," said Bill. "You'll hear of it yourself soon, I guess, from Miss Milly or Mr. Rutherford; but I got first word of it."

"What is it?" asked Jim.

"You're goin' to school; you and Theodore Yorke," said Bill.

"I ain't goin' to no school with Theodore Yorke," interrupted Jim. "There ain't no school would hold me an' him."

"Yes, you are, if you know what's good for yourself," said Bill; "and there's some kind of a big prize for whichever comes out best man."

"Then I'll go, if Miss Milly lets me; an' beat him, too, if it was just for the sake of beatin'," said Jim, verifying the prophecy of his young mistress. "But how do you know so much, an' what do you mean, Bill?"

"I didn't hear all they was sayin', and I s'pose I wasn't meant to hear none of it," answered Bill. "It was all the fam'ly folks, 'cept the children, was talkin'. Mr. Brady sent me to open the front-door when the bell rang, and it was some flowers for Miss Amy; and, when I went to the door with 'em, they was all talkin' so busy they didn't hear me knock. I couldn't make out just what it all was; but you're to get schoolin', you and Theodore, and whichever does the best is to get more schoolin', and some prize at the end when the schoolin's done; but Miss Milly, she didn't want you nor him to know you was fightin' for it, 'cause she didn't think 'twould be good for *you.* She thought you'd be too set on it, maybe, just to spite Theodore. She knows him and you, you see."

" Yes, she might ha' knowed I wouldn't let *him* get the best of me," said Jim, viciously. " And you say I wasn't to be let know I was set on to beat him."

" No, them was Miss Milly's orders; and I take it Mr. Rutherford didn't like it too much," answered Bill. " He wanted you to know, and be set on yer mettle. But Miss Milly, she's boss of *us,* you know, and she got her own way. So, as I say, they ain't goin' to tell you nothin' about Theodore."

" Then, maybe you oughtn't to ha' told me," said Jim, musingly. " I don't believe you ought."

" I don't see the harm," said Bill. " I wasn't told not to tell; they didn't know I heard."

" All the same," said Jim, " you oughtn't to ha' told, when Miss Milly didn't want me to know. I am glad I do know, so as I can set out to beat Theodore; and, Bill, this is goin' to give me a first-rate chance. You see if I don't get to be President, now. An', when I do, you'll see what'll be done to Theodore Yorke."

" What ? " asked Bill.

" I don' know, I've got to think," answered Jim ; " but jus' you wait till I get to be top man of these States. Won't Theodore get it ! "

"Miss Milly didn't want you to know, 'cause she thought you'd be so set against him, and she thought you was bad enough that way a'ready," said Bill.

"I feel kinder sneaky to know it when she didn't want me to," said Jim. "I guess, after all, I'm sorry you tole me, Bill; you hadn't a right to, I guess. You come by it yourself kinder listenin'."

Here the question of conscience and honor was broken in upon by the coachman, who slept in an adjoining room, and who bade the boys cease their chattering, as they disturbed him.

Uncle Rutherford had left to Milly the telling of his plans for Jim's future; and the following morning she called the boy to her, and set them forth before him.

He was to go to school this winter, beginning as soon as the Christmas holidays were over. With many earnest warnings, she pressed upon him the necessity for self-control, as well as attention to his studies; telling him of the prize to be won if his course should prove satisfactory to Mr. Rutherford, but making no mention, of course, of the other candidate. He promised over and over again, that he would do his very best to prove a credit to her, and to make her "awful proud" of him in the future, and that she should have no cause for complaint, either with his temper, or his lack of diligence.

That he was enchanted with the opportunity thus offered to him, there could be no doubt, but he did not appear as much surprised as Milly imagined that he would be; and there was something in his manner, which, at the time, struck Milly as rather strange, — a something repressed, as it were, but excited; and, all the while, there was a gleam of mischief in his eye. In the light of later developments, the cause of this was made plain; but now it was a mystery.

"And now, Jim," continued his young mistress, when she had told him of all that lay within his grasp, and had added a gentle and persuasive modicum of moral suasion, — "now that you are going out into the world to make a way, it may be a name, for yourself, you must choose what that name shall be. You remember," soothingly, for this was a sore point with the boy, — "you remember that we know you only as Jim."

"It's Livin'stone, Jim — no, I mean James Rutherford Livin'stone," said the boy, decidedly. "I'm goin' to put in the Rutherford on account of Mr. Rutherford bein' so good to me, Miss Milly; an' won't you an' him be set up when you see Rutherford Livin'stone names onto a President of these States? I ain't never goin' to disgrace them names, that I ain't."

But Milly, mindful of the prejudices of her relatives, and of the objections which she foresaw from both sides of the family, found it needful to decline the compliment. In order to avoid hurting the boy's pride, however, she went about it most diplomatically.

"Do you not think, Jim," she said, "that it would be a good thing for you to call yourself by the name of Washington, the first and greatest of our Presidents?"

"Jim George Washington, Miss Milly?" answered the lad. "Well, that would sound nice; but, you see, I wanted to put the compliment on *you*, an' to show what lots of gratitude I've got for you an' your folks, Miss Milly."

"The best compliment you could pay to me, and to my care for you, Jim, would be to show yourself in any way worthy of bearing the name of that great and good man," said Milly, non-plussed how to carry her point, and still not to wound her charge. "And," she continued, "that name might always prove a reminder to you of the truth and uprightness, the bravery and self-control, which distinguished him."

"Miss Milly," Jim broke forth, irrelevantly, it would seem, "you know Bill gets time for lots of readin' an' studyin' down at the office. When Mr. Edward don't have any thin' for him to do, an' he might be just loafin' round, he's doin' his 'rithmetic, or his jography or spellin', an,' if he wants a bit of help, Mr. Edward gives it to him, if he ain't *too* busy just then; so Bill, he's comin' on with his learnin' heaps faster than me; he's gettin' splendid at figgers, an' he reads the paper, too, on'y Mr. Edward, he don't like him to read the murders an' the hangin's, and them *very* interestin' things ; but Bill read the other day in the paper how a man said George Washington had a big temper, an' could get as mad — as mad as any thin'. But Bill, he said he'd heard Mr. Edward an' some other gentleman talkin' 'bout how folks was always tryin' now to be upsettin' of hist'ry ; an' Bill says he reckons that 'bout George Washington was just another upsettin', an' him an' me ain't goin' to believe it."

"That's right, Jim, keep your faith in Washington, and show that you do so by adopting his name," said Milly.

Do not let it be thought that Milly slighted the Father of her country, by thus turning over to him the "compliment" she declined for herself and her family ; for, in the multitude of namesakes who have helped to perpetuate that illustrious memory, poor Jim could reflect but an infinitesimal share of credit or discredit.

Jim pondered. The advantages of the world-renowned historic cognomen were, doubtless, great. But the "compliment" to his friends ! could he defraud them of that ?

Suddenly his face lighted ; a brilliant idea had struck him. He could combine both.

"Miss Milly," he said, "I'll tell you. Now, I'll be named James Rutherford Livin'stone Washin'ton, an' stick to that till I get inter President polyticks ; then I'll put the Livin'stone last, James Rutherford Washin'ton Livin'stone, so folks'll be sure I belong to you. Bill says folks can change their names, if they has a mind to, when they come twenty-one. Bill's learned lots of law down to Wall Street, Miss Milly ; he's up in it, I can tell you."

"Very well, that will be best," said Milly, content to defer to the doubtful future the risk of having the family names appear in " President polyticks ; " and so it was arranged, and her charge prepared to face the world as James Washington.

CHAPTER VII.

TWO PEANUT-VENDERS.

CHAPTER VII.

TWO PEANUT-VENDERS.

ALLIE stood before the glorious wood fire, around which we were all gathered awaiting the summons to dinner, gazing intently into its glowing depths, and evidently sunk in such deep meditation as to be oblivious, for the moment, of her surroundings, and of what she was doing; for her doll, a new and much prized Christmas-gift from uncle Rutherford, and a beauty, hung disregarded, head downwards, in the hand which had sunk unconsciously by her side, while, with the forefinger of the other pressed upon her rosy little lips, she seemed to be pondering some weighty matter.

Daisy lay stretched with her doll upon the tiger-skin, and presently, looking up, roused Allie from her distraction.

"Why, Allie," she exclaimed, "what you finking about so much? Serena Victoria is most upside down. Just look at her!"

Allie reversed her doll to its proper position; and, as she settled its costume, gave Daisy her answer, by putting into words the thought which was vexing the minds of some of her elders, but addressed herself to me, as a kindred spirit.

"Amy, do you b'lieve Mrs. Yorke will be very fit-to-be-seen to take out walking or driving on the avenue, or in the park?"

"Why, Allie," I said, weakly evading the question, and also answering by another, "do you not think your friend Mrs. Yorke is always fit to be seen?"

Still, Allie replied by a fresh query.

"Amy, have you seen Mrs. Yorke's best bonnet? her 'sabbath bonnet,' she calls it." And she turned upon me large eyes, full of solemn meaning.

Yes, I had, indeed, seen Mrs. Yorke's "sabbath bonnet;" and it was the recollection of that appalling article of attire which at the present moment was weighing on my own spirits.

Here Daisy piped up, also giving voice to the sentiments of her sisters.

"Mrs. Yorke is very nice," she said, "and we love her lots, but in her Sunday clothes she don't seem like Mrs. Yorke."

It was even so. Mrs. Yorke in her every-day costume, and Mrs. Yorke in gorgeous Sunday array, were two — and "oh the difference to me!"

"How do you know," said uncle Rutherford, "but that Santa Claus himself may have taken the matter in hand? Mrs. Yorke's Sunday bonnet may not have been to his taste, and he may have provided her with another."

"I hope, then," answered Allie, sceptically, "that he hasn't brought her a brown felt with red feathers and a terra-cotta bow."

"That would not have improved matters much, would it?" asked uncle Rutherford, with a twinkle in his eye. "No; I think his taste would run to black, perhaps. What do you say, aunt Emily?"

"I should say his fancy would lie in a black felt, with black velvet trimmings and feathers," answered aunt Emily. "How would that do, Allie?"

"Very well," said Allie, "if he brought her a black dress, too, 'stead of a' old plaid."

"And a new cloak, too," put in Daisy. "Her's isn't very pretty; I saw it once; but I'd just as lieve have Mrs. Yorke anyhow she was."

The grammar might be childishly faulty, but the feeling of the speech was without a flaw, and from the heart Daisy would have accepted Mrs. Yorke as she was, and thought it no shame or embarrassment to escort her anywhere; but bonny Allie was a lady of high degree, with an eye for appearances and the proprieties, and Mrs. Yorke's antiquated and incongruous gala costume would sorely have tried her soul, although she would doubtless have borne her company with a good grace, and with no outward show of the pangs she might be enduring. How greatly she was relieved now could be judged by the laughing light which sparkled in her eyes, the dimples which showed themselves at the corners of her mouth, and the ecstatic way in which she hugged the long-suffering doll.

"She'll be lovely and fit-to-be-seen now!" she exclaimed. "Won't she, Daisy? She'll look just like mammy."

"But," said Daisy, doubtfully, unconscious of the knowing gaze which her older little sister had fixed upon uncle Rutherford's face, a gaze which he returned with interest — "but *did* Santa Claus bring Mrs. Yorke all those things, Allie?"

"Yes, he did; *a* Santa Claus did; I'm perfectly sure he did," said Allie. "But they didn't come in her stocking, or grow on a Christmas-tree, either, *I* know."

"I fink he was real mean if he brought her all those, and didn't bring her a muff and some gloves and a' umbulla, too," said Daisy.

Before the laugh, which followed, had subsided, Thomas appeared at one entrance to announce dinner, and mammy at the other to carry off her charges. Full of the news they had to impart to her, of Santa Claus's supposed benefactions to Mrs. Yorke, they went more willingly than usual.

Yes, Christmas had come and gone, — Christmas with all its sacred, hallowed associations, its pastimes and pleasures, its loving remembrances and family gatherings; and never had a dearer and happier one been passed beneath our roof. No, nor one more productive of choice and beautiful gifts from each one to each; and the little ones had outdone themselves for the blessed and beloved holiday.

And it was an article of the family creed, both on the Livingstone and Rutherford sides, that the good things which had been so bountifully showered upon our pathway in life should be shared with others, especially at this season of peace and good-will. So it was no surprise, although it was a great relief to some of us, to learn that Mrs. Yorke had been made presentable for the visit to the city, which would involve some attentions on our part that might have proved embarrassing had she appeared in her wonted holiday costume. Mother and aunt Emily had been the two good fairies who had wrought the transformation through the medium of a Christmas-box, which had contained bountiful gifts for the whole Yorke family.

And now Captain and Mrs. Yorke were to come to the city on the very next day, accompanied by the — to Jim, at least — objectionable Theodore. Mrs. Yorke, whose crippled condition sadly interfered with her comfort and usefulness in life, was to be placed immediately under the care of our own family physician, who had become interested in her case during a visit paid to us at the seashore during the previous summer; and aunt Emily had secured a comfortable abiding-place for her, not very far from our own home, where the children, whom she adored, and mammy could often run in to see her, and where the elder members of the family could now and then pay her a visit. The captain was to remain with her, or not, as his inclination might prompt; but uncle Rutherford thought, that, the novelty of city sights and sounds once exhausted, the old man would prefer to return to his accustomed haunts by the sea. Theodore was to board with his grandparents, and to begin school with the New Year; at the same time, and — alas! for the inexpediency of uncle Rutherford's arrangements — in the same school, with Jim.

Such were the plans which had been made for the Yorkes, and the junior portion of our household were in a state of eager expectation over their approaching arrival; the desire to witness the old seaman's first impressions of a city life, and his own conduct therein, being strong within us.

"We'll give him a good time, and get lots of fun out of it for ourselves," said Norman and Douglas, who proposed to be his pioneers.

As for Bill and Jim, there was no telling what manner of projects they might have formed for his edification, and their own amusement and his; and father considered it necessary to bid Milly give them a word of warning not to practise on the credulity of the old sailor, as they had at times been wont to do while we were at the seashore.

"And what about the mercantile enterprise of that youth, with so many irons in the fire?" asked uncle Rutherford, when dinner was over, and the door closed behind the retreating servants, while we still lingered around the table; the little girls having been allowed to come down to dessert. "How does the peanut-business flourish, Milly? You are posted, I suppose."

"Not so thoroughly as Allie and Daisy," answered Milly. "I understand that it is flourishing; but, if you wish for minute particulars, you must apply to them."

Allie, hearing what was passing, forthwith dived into the depths of her small pocket, and produced from thence a miniature account-book, saying triumphantly as she did so, —

"Jim's sold the first bag of peanuts, and bought another, and then sold that; and now he's bought *two* at once, and "—opening the book, and poring over it, —"and he's made—see, uncle Rutherford, here it is," and she pointed out a row of crooked, childish, illegible figures; to be understood, doubtless, by the initiated, but Greek to uncle Rutherford.

"How does the boy manage to keep account of his business?" asked uncle Rutherford, returning the book to Allie, as wise as when she handed it to him, but not confessing his ignorance.

"By preparing himself for a dyspeptic existence," said Milly. "He swallows his meals in haste, Thomas says, and rushes from the table, and around to the Fourth Avenue to receive Tony's report, and be back in time for his work. Nor is he always quite in time, I imagine; but Thomas is indulgent and patient, and Bill helps him. I understand that the little cripples are really making fair sales, and Jim is reaping quite a harvest."

"Yes, uncle Rutherford knows that by my 'count-book," said unsuspicious Allie. "Read it aloud, please, uncle, so they can all hear."

"Hm — hm, yes, my dear; but I do not like to read aloud after dinner," said uncle Rutherford, still forbearing to enlighten her innocence.

"It isn't so *much* reading," murmured Allie, rather hurt, for she was an over-sensitive child, prone to imagine slights, and, as we know, given to ready tears. "I'll tell you, people;" and she proceeded to give the amount made by Jim since he had established the peanut-stand, with its various divisions for the separate objects of his benevolence and ambition. The latter figured under the head of "For to be President;" and if her accounts, or, rather, Jim's as set down by her, were to be trusted, he had really done very well in the stand business.

"We know two deforms," quoth Daisy, solemnly, as Allie closed; "one deform is very nice and good, and the ofer is horrid and scratching. One is Captain Yorke's, and the ofer is Jim's peanut-stand girl. But we have to be good to the cross deform, 'cause God made her that way. Allie and I are going to try and make her nice and pleasant, too."

"She thinks we're proud, and only like to go to see her, and show her our nice dolls and things, to make her feel sorry," said Allie; "Tony said so. And she turns her hump at us, and makes faces at us, and *won't* think we want to be good to her. She thinks we're proud at her, 'cause she has to sell peanuts."

"You go and sell peanuts, then, and show her you're not too proud to do it," said Douglas, carelessly, and certainly with no thought that the suggestion would ever be acted upon.

"We needn't to have been afraid about Mrs. Yorke's fit-to-be-seenedness," said Allie, hopping delightedly around on one foot, the day after the arrival of the Yorkes, and on her return from her first visit to them. "Why, she does look so nice; just as nice as mammy in her Sunday clothes. She looks almost lady."

"Yes, she does, and it don't make any dif'ence, if she *behaves* lady," said Daisy; "and I fink she always behaves *very* lady. Mamma," with a sudden and startling change of subject, "if somebody told you you could do somefing to help somebody, oughtn't you to do it?"

"Yes, my darling, if you can," answered mother, rather oblivious, to tell the truth, of the child's earnestness in putting the question; for she was at the moment writing an answer to a note which had been just brought in.

"And it's very nice to do the kind fing, and not speak about it, isn't it?" questioned Daisy.

"Very, dear," answered mother, still only half hearing the little one, and far from thinking that she was supposed to be giving her sanction to a most unheard of proceeding.

Mrs. Yorke's attire and general appearance proved satisfactory even to fastidious Miss Allie and myself; indeed, she would have passed muster among any hundred elderly women of the respectable middle class; and there was nothing whatever about her to attract special attention, unless one turned again for a second look at the kind, motherly old face. There was a sort of natural refinement about her, too, which made her adapt herself with some ease to her unaccustomed surroundings.

As for the captain, he was a hopeless subject for those who had an eye to fashion or the commonplace. No amount of attempts at smoothing or trimming him down, no efforts at personal adornment in his case, could make of him any thing but what he was, here in the great city, as well as at his seaside home, the typical old sea-faring man, rough, hearty, simple, and good-natured, garrulous to excess, as we had often proved, and not to be polished, or made what he called "cityfied."

"'Tain't no sort of use whitewashin' the old hulk," he asserted; "an' I guess my Sunday clo's, as is good enough for the Lord's meetin'-house up to the Pint, is got to be good enough for these messed-up city streets; an' ye can't make no bricky-bracky outer me."

To the boys he was a source of unmixed delight, both to our own young brothers, and to the two servant-lads; and no care for the eyes or comments of the world troubled any one of them when he happened to be under their escort. And little Daisy was equally independent, or perhaps too innocent to take any heed of such matters.

A feverish, influenza cold confined both Allie and mammy to the house for a day or two soon after the arrival of the Yorkes in the city, and Daisy was consequently obliged to be confided to the care of others when she took her walks.

She had been out driving one afternoon with mother and aunt Emily; and they, having an engagement for "a tea," to which they could not take her, brought her home. At the foot of our front-steps stood Captain Yorke, complacently basking in the almost April sunshine, and amusing himself by gazing up and down the street, and across the park, on which our house fronted. It was an exceptionally beautiful day for the time of year, soft, balmy, and springlike.

"Ye won't git another like it to-morrer; two sich don't come together this time o' year," said the captain, as mother, greeting him, remarked on the loveliness of the weather. "Ye kin look out for a gale to close out the year with, I reckon. There's mischief brewin' over yonder," pointing to where a bank of clouds lay low upon the south-western horizon. "Ye'd best take yer fill of bein' out doors to-day."

"Yes," said Daisy, pleadingly, "it's so nice and pleasant. Mamma, couldn't some of the servants take me out a little more? I don't want to go in yet."

"Leave her along of me, Mis' Livin'stone," said the old man. "Me an' her'll take care of one another."

Daisy beamed at the proposition; and mother had not the heart to refuse her, or the old sailor.

"Well," she said, "you may stay out a while with the captain; but only on condition that you both promise not to go far from the house, but remain either on the Square, or on this block. You see, captain," she continued, "Daisy is too little to pilot you about, and you are too much of a stranger in the city to be a guide for her beyond the neighborhood of home. If you want to leave her, or she tires, just take her to the door, and ring the bell for her. Or perhaps you will go in yourself, and see Allie and mammy. — They cannot go astray or get into any trouble so near home," she said to aunt Emily, when she had given her orders, and the carriage moved on, leaving Daisy and the captain standing side by side on the pavement, the little one with her tiny hand clasped in the toil-worn palm of the veteran.

"Impossible!" said aunt Emily; "and the captain is as good as any nurse, you know. I would quite as soon trust her with him as with mammy."

But aunt Emily, and mother too, had forgotten to take into account the captain's deficiency of a sense of the fitness of things, — at least, of matters appertaining to a city-life.

He and Daisy rambled contentedly up and down the block, from one corner to another, for some time, she prattling away to him, and enlightening his ignorance so far as she was able, until, at last, they unfortunately touched upon Jim's affairs.

"Let's go round an' buy some peanuts outer Jim's stand," said the captain. "'Tain't far, ye know."

"No," answered obedient Daisy, "not far; but mamma said we mustn't go way from sight of our house, fear we would be lost, and we'd be way from sight of it if we went to Jim's peanut-stand. But, Captain Yorke, Matty is cross wif Allie and me, 'cause she finks we're proud 'cause we don't sell peanuts; and Douglas says I ought to sell peanuts, so she'll know I'm not proud. Do you fink we could sell a few peanuts now? I know where Jim keeps 'em."

"Wal, I reckon ye kin sell peanuts, my pretty, if ye have 'em to sell," answered the old man, seeing no reason why Daisy should not have her own way, and perhaps scenting a little diversion for himself in the project; "but if ye can't go round to t'other street, how are ye goin' to get 'em ?"

"Oh, Jim keeps 'em — his bags of peanuts — out in a pantry under our back-stoop," said Daisy; "and ev'y morning Tony comes for some to sell. We'll go in, and ask some of the servants to give us some, and then we'll sell 'em."

If "some of the servants" had been found, this unprecedented plan would have met with due interference; but it so happened, that they were all scattered at their various avocations in different parts of the house, and none were in the kitchen save old Mary Jane, to whom Daisy knew better than to appeal on behalf of any interests of Jim's. She was busy grinding coffee; and the noise of the mill prevented her from hearing the footsteps of the invaders of her domain, who passed through the basement-hall, and out of the back-door, where, although they found no one to help them, Daisy, to her great delight, discovered the key of the closet in the lock. To open the door, bid the captain take down an empty basket, which hung on a hook, and to fill this with peanuts from an

"TWO RATHER UNUSUAL FIGURES TO BE ENGAGED IN SUCH AN OCCUPATION."—*Page* 145.

open bag, was but the work of a few moments; the captain's huge hands scooping up the nuts in quantities, and soon accomplishing the task. Then, arming themselves with a tin cup, which they also found near at hand, by way of a measure, the two conspirators once more stole past the unconscious Mary Jane, and out into the street, the captain bearing the basket.

"Shall we sell 'em on our stoop?" asked Daisy, all this time quite guiltless of any intention of wrong-doing.

"I reckon ye'd best go down to the corner there, where the two streets comes together," answered the captain, pointing to where a much-frequented cross-street intersected our avenue. "Them's my opinions, for I see lots more folks walkin' that way than this."

Unfortunately, Daisy saw the force of his reasoning; and the two innocents had presently established themselves, quite to their own satisfaction, on this public corner.

It was not long before they attracted sufficient attention, for they were two rather unusual looking figures to be engaged in such an occupation, to say nothing of the contrast between them; the weather-beaten, rugged, by no means handsome old sailor standing guard, as it were, over the daintily dressed little child with her beautiful, beaming face, and winning ways.

Custom flowed in without delay, the captain not

hesitating to hail the passers-by, and to direct their attention to the tiny saleswoman before him; while she, with her sweet voice, pleading, "Please buy some peanuts to help some poor children;" and her attractive air and appearance was irresistible.

Fortunately for the pecuniary interests of the firm, or, rather, of the capitalist whom they represented, Daisy knew from the boys the price that the peanuts should be; and the captain, who, spite of his simplicity, had a keen eye to business, and who was accustomed to peddling about "the Point" during the summer season, constituted himself cash-taker, and saw that she received her dues.

But public curiosity was naturally excited by the unusual situation, and presently both Daisy and Captain Yorke were besieged with questions, which the latter resented as implying a distrust of his ability to care for the child. Truly, it might well be doubted. But this was no check upon custom, and the stock in the basket at Daisy's feet speedily dwindled down. The bottom had nearly been reached, when a policeman sauntered by on the other side of the street; and, being attracted by the gathering on the corner, — for those who came to buy, in many cases remained to admire, — he crossed over to ascertain the cause. Great was his astonishment, and small his approbation, when he discovered the state of things ; for he knew our children by sight, and could not but be aware that such doings as these could not be with the approbation of Daisy's family.

"Why, that is — isn't that Mr. Livingstone's little girl?" he asked of the captain.

The captain nodded ; he was too busily engaged in keeping an eye on the money Daisy received, to do more.

"Well, if ever I saw a thing like this!" ejaculated the guardian of the peace. "To see a little lady like that — my dear, do your pa and ma know what you're a doing?"

"No, not yet," answered Daisy ; who looked with cordial eye upon all policemen, as being, according to her code, the defenders of the right, and avengers of the wrong. — "No, not yet ; I'll tell them by and by, and they'll be glad, 'cause they like me to do a kindness, and not speak about it."

"*Will* they?" said the policeman, with a clearer insight into the fitness of things, than was possessed by Daisy or the old sailor. "Now, my little lady, you've got to go straight home ; I know what your pa and ma will say. You come right along home, like a good child."

"Now, you let her alone," interposed Captain Yorke. "'Tain't no case for the law, 'sposin' her folks don't like it ; an' I'll wager they do."

"You old lunatic," said the policeman, "what

are you encouragin' of her for ? Who ever saw a little lady like that sellin' peanuts in the streets ! I ain't goin' to allow it nohow; it's drawin' a crowd ; and, as to the law, she nor you ain't any right to be sellin' 'em here without a license. — Come along home, little Miss."

But here a new actor appeared upon the scene, and prevented any further opposition on the part of the captain. This was Jim, who was returning from an errand ; and, seeing Captain Yorke's tall figure standing by the lamp-post with an unmis- takably belligerent expression in every line, he elbowed his way through the fast increasing crowd, and stood astonished and dismayed before Daisy.

"Miss Daisy, whatever do you mean by this ? You sellin' peanuts here in the street !"

"Matty Blair does," faltered Daisy, beginning, by virtue of all these various protests, to see that perhaps she might have strayed from the way in which she should go.

"Matty Blair !" ejaculated Jim, again. "Well, Miss Daisy, I guess Matty Blair's one, an' you're another. Won't your pa an' ma, an' all of 'em, be mad, though !"

"So I was sayin'," said the policeman, who was quite well acquainted with Jim ; "and now, young- ster, the best thing you can do is to take the little lady home, and tell her folks to look out for her better than to put her under the care of this old know-nothing."

This entirely met Jim's views; and, snatching up the almost empty basket, he seized the hand of the now frightened Daisy, and hurried her homeward, leaving the policeman and the captain exchanging compliments until such time as the latter saw fit to retire from the field, and hasten to our house to deliver up the results of poor Daisy's sale.

It may be imagined what consternation reigned in the Livingstone household, when this escapade of its youngest member came to light; while the grief and bewilderment of that little damsel herself, who had, in all good faith, believed that she had mother's sanction for her course, were pitiable to witness. As for Jim, not even the gratifying pecuniary results could nullify his mortification at the disgrace which he believed to have fallen upon the family, especially his beloved Miss Daisy; and he found it hard to forgive the captain, who had encouraged and abetted her.

"Philanthropy has certainly seized upon this family to an alarming extent," said Bessie Sandford, when she heard the story, "but I *wish* that I had been there to see pet Daisy at her post acting peanut-vender."

How far Daisy's effort to prove to Matty that she "was not proud" affected that young cripple, could not be told; but she did not fail to hear of the thing from Jim.

As for Captain Yorke, he received his full share

of reprimand, and caution for the future, from his wife, who, all unaccustomed as she, too, was to city ways, had far more natural sense of what was fitting and advisable.

"If I could but go round with him to keep him up to the mark, Mrs. Livingstone," she said, when apologizing to mother for the captain's share in the late escapade; "but, bless you, dear lady, he's more of a child than little Daisy herself, when he's out of his usual bearings. I think he's best off at home, with Jabez and Matildy Jane to look after him, when I can't."

And she sighed heavily, as if the responsibility were too much for her.

But the captain could not be brought to this view of the case. He was enjoying himself in his own way among the city sights and sounds.

CHAPTER VIII.

NOT ON THE PROGRAMME.

CHAPTER VIII.

UNCLE RUTHERFORD stood at the far end of the
great schoolroom, awaiting the admission of his
two candidates for its privileges and opportunities.
It was the opening-day after the conclusion of the
Christmas holidays ; and half a dozen boys, besides
Theodore Yorke and Jim, had presented themselves as new scholars, and they now stood before
the principal, — Theodore at one end of the line,
and Jim at the other.

"What is your name?" asked the principal of
Theodore ; to which the boy responded simply,
"Theodore Yorke," and then answered in like
manner the few more questions put to him relative
to age and so forth ; and the gentleman passed
down the line till he came to Jim.

"What is your name?"

To uncle Rutherford's consternation, Jim,
straightening himself up, answered in a loud,
confident tone, "Jim," — he had meant to say
"James," but the more familiar appellation
escaped him, — "Jim Grant Garfield Rutherford
Livingstone Washington;" and then glanced

down the line as if to say, "Beat that if you can!"

A titter ran around the room, speedily checked by the stern eye of the principal, and one or two of the new boys giggled outright; but Jim, with head erect, and fearless eyes fixed upon the master, was unmoved, perhaps did not even guess that the merriment was caused by himself.

The principal found it necessary to caress his whiskers a little, then said, —

"Good names, my boy, every one of them. Try to prove worthy to bear them. Your age?"

This and the other needful preliminaries being settled, the new boys were turned over to the examiners, to have their classes and position in the school defined; and uncle Rutherford made his exit, only too thankful that the irrepressible Jim had not added to his list of high-sounding appellations, "President that is to be of these United States."

School discipline, of course, had, for the time, restrained the gibes and sneers, the open laugh, which would have greeted Jim's announcement of his adopted name or names; but the time was only deferred. The joke was, to the schoolboy mind, too good to be lost; and when the recess came, and the boys were for a while at liberty, Jim became the target for many sorry witticisms, and "Jim Grant Garfield Rutherford Livingstone Washington" was called from all sides of the playground in almost as many tones of mockery as there were boys; and Jim speedily found that he had taken too much upon himself for his own comfort. The "Grant Garfield" had been an after-thought, and he had been prompted thereto by hearing another boy give his name — to which he was probably justly entitled — as "George William Winfield Scott Jones." Jim was not going to be outdone, or to be satisfied with four names, when here was a fellow with five; hence the "Grant Garfield" on the spur of the moment.

Milly had feared that even the "Rutherford Livingstone Washington" would excite derisive comment; and when she heard uncle Rutherford's report of Jim's further adoption of great names, she groaned in spirit, and awaited with sundry apprehensions his return from school, fearing that his excitable temper might have been provoked into some manifestation, which would not only affect his creditable entrance into the school, but also his standing with uncle Rutherford.

But Jim had a check upon himself whereof Milly wot not; namely, that he knew of the prize to be secured in case he gained the approbation of uncle Rutherford, — a prize which, as we know, he was more anxious to win for the sake of defeating Theodore Yorke than for the attainment of the scholarship itself.

So, although he had to put a strong restraint upon himself, and was inwardly boiling with wrath and indignation, he bore the gibes and sneers with the utmost self-command, and apparently unfailing good-nature, till Theodore Yorke, who had made himself at home among his new surroundings as readily as Jim had done, joined in the "chaffing" with a vim and bitterness which could have their source only in a feeling of personal spite and hatred.

"Jim Grant Garfield Rutherford Livingstone Washington," he repeated; "and he hasn't a right to *one* of the names, unless it's Jim. He hasn't got any name; nobody knows what his name is, or who he is, or where he came from. He hasn't got any folks, either."

This was wounding poor Jim in the tenderest point, as the amiable Theodore well knew; and it was more than his victim could well stand.

"And I'd rather have no folks at all than have such as yours," he shouted, almost beside himself with rage at this exposure of that which he con- sidered to be his disgrace. Then suddenly recalled to a sense of his regard for this boy's grand- parents, Captain and Mrs. Yorke, and of all the kindness he had received from them, — for a hearty gratitude for favors received was one of the strongest features of Jim's character, — he has- tened to set matters in their true light; "at least, such a father as they tell yours was. If I had a gran'father or gran'mother like yours, there couldn't be none better; but if I had a father was such a scallywag as yours, I say a good sight better have none. And you ain't a bit like the old folks, neither; you're another such a one as your father. *I* wouldn't own such a one!"

This tirade was interspersed with other expressions more forcible than choice, and which are better omitted; and, as may be supposed, it did not tend to mend matters. Recrimination followed recrimination; insults from one to another went from bad to worse, Theodore being even more of an adept in such language than Jim, who had always been considered a proficient; and one of the teachers came upon the playground just in time to see Jim deal a furious blow at his opponent, who caught sight of the master before he had returned it, which he would otherwise doubtless have done; and who immediately assumed an air of innocent, injured virtue, too lofty-minded and forgiving to return the blow.

As the rules against fighting within school bounds were particularly severe, Jim's was a heinous offence. He was sternly called to order and reprimanded with severity; and although, in consideration of his being a new boy, he was let off with this, he began his school career somewhat under a cloud; while Theodore posed as a martyr, and a boy with a regard for school discipline, — to his teachers, — but the other boys knew better, and with few exceptions espoused Jim's cause, and at once pronounced Theodore the "sneak" and "bully" that he was.   But that was small comfort to Jim, who, on coming home, had to report, as he truthfully did, that he had failed to keep his temper on this the very first day of his entrance into the school.

Milly consoled and encouraged him as best she might, bidding him to take heart and to struggle even harder for the future, and being very sparing of blame for his share in the quarrel.

Fate, as short-sighted and with as dull an eye to expediency as uncle Rutherford, had decreed not only that the two boys, Jim and Theodore, should be in the same school, but, their attainments being of about the same range, that they should be put into the same class, an arrangement which did not tend to the maintenance of the peace so much to be desired.

But, in spite of his unlucky beginning, Jim speedily became a favorite in the school, both with masters and schoolmates.   His frank, merry ways, obliging disposition, ready wit, and quickness at repartee, soon gained him a host of friends on the playground; while his evident desire to make progress in his studies, — wherein he had a stimulus unsuspected by any one but Bill, — his sturdy truthfulness, and general obedience to rules and regulations, won him golden opinions from those in authority.   Ambition, whether for greater or lesser aims, was Jim's ruling passion, and now he had so many spurs to urge him on; for, added to his own personal aspirations and the determination to prove himself a credit to his benefactors, was the overwhelming desire to outstrip Theodore, and wrest from him the prize.

Milly noticed, whenever he reported progress to her, that there was a certain sort of repressed excitability about him, a wistful nervousness very foreign to his assured independence and self-confidence, and he several times seemed as if he were going to make some disclosure to her; all of which made his young mistress think that he had something on his mind which he was half inclined to impart to her, although he could not quite resolve to do so. She bided her time, however, being sure that it would come sooner or later, and only now and then tried to open the way by asking him if he had any thing further to tell her.

But the only result of this would be a shame-faced embarrassment and a sheepish denial, followed by an evident desire to cut short the interview.

When Jim had been at school about a month, making, according to the reports of his teachers, who were closely questioned by uncle Rutherford, fair progress with his studies, and showing a self-command and control over his temper which had not been expected from him after the fiery outburst of the first day, an incident occurred which would have afforded him an opportunity for mortifying Theodore, had he not been restrained by a motive which was stronger than his antagonism to his rival.

The vagaries and peculiarities of Captain Yorke, with his ignorance and indifference to city ways and manners, had more than once drawn public notice upon him ; the episode of Daisy as a peanut-vender, with the old sailor as her aider and abetter, being but a trifling circumstance compared to some others ; and Mrs. Yorke was in constant terror lest he should in some way make himself more notorious than would prove agreeable.

About this time, a celebrated actor was performing in the city in the farce of " Dundreary Married," wherein Lord Dundreary having, as the title indicates, taken to himself a wife, falls beneath the tyranny of a domineering mother-in-law, to whom he submits till submission becomes intolerable, when he turns upon her, asserts himself, and proclaims himself master in his own house.

Our boys, Norman and Douglas, having seen the farce in company with the rest of the family, and having been greatly amused by it, conceived the idea of treating the captain to a sight of the same ; and, having obtained father's permission to do so, they invited the old man to an evening's entertainment.

" Wa'al," he drawled with his usual deliberation when considering any matter, " I don' care if I do. When I was a youngster, I was brung up to

think play-actin' was a sin, an' I'd about as soon
a thought of shakin' han's with the evil one hisself, as of goin' to the theayter; but either I've
gotten wiser as I've gotten older, or else maybe
the play-actin' folks has gotten better behaved;
but times is changed somehow, an' I seen some
play-actin' in the hotel down to the P'int, an' they
was real ladies an' gentlemen did it, too. I was a
peepin' in at the winders more'n once; an' the
hotel-keepers, Mr. Loydd an' Mr. Field, if they
didn't come, one one time, an' t'other another, an'
bring me into the hall an' near to the doors where
I could see fust-rate. An' I didn't see no harm
onto it. The play-actors was very pretty behaved,
an' I didn't see no breakin' of comman'ments. I
never could see what folks wanted to purtend they
was other folks for, and sometimes to go a-talkin'
as if they was come out of by-gone days. But if
you're for takin' me to the theayter, I reckon I
won't come to no harm by it. Enyhow, I know
ye've got to come to city ways when ye're to the
city; folks kinder look daggers at ye ef ye don't.
There's the landlady to the house where me and
Mis' Yorke puts up; she's the best, an allers doin'
for Mis' Yorke, an' come an' sit with her an' talk
—my talk by the hour she will, straight on, like
as she'd been woun' up; an' she come yesterday,
all kin' of fussy like, an' her face red, an' she
says, says she, 'Captain Yorke,' says she, 'ef ye
wouldn't mind me askin' a little favor of ye?'"

"'Sartinly not, ma'am,' says I; an' I was reckonin' she was wantin' to borrer money. But what
do ye s'pose it was, Norman? She goes and she
says, says she, kinder hesitatin' like yet, 'Would
ye mind, capt'in, a-eatin' with yer fork, 'stead of
yer knife? Miss Jarvis, what sits next ye at the
table, she's kinder narvous, an' she says it sets
her teeth on edge, an' she says she can't stan' it;
an' she's my best payin' boarder, bein' she has the
second-story front an' back; an' it would obleege
me, ef ye don't min'.'

"'Jes' as lief eat off ten forks, ma'am,' says I,
'ef it suits ye an' Mis' Jarvis. I been a-noticin'
she was kinder pernikity like an' fussy, an' kinder
offish with me; but if it's the difference of knives
or forks, the best payin' boarder ain't goin' to be
hurt by me.' But, boys! I didn't know by a long
shot what I was a-promisin'. I tell ye, the knife
would keep goin' up the nateral way as it was
used to; an' yesterday I didn't get no kind of a
dinner, nor a breakfast this mornin', thinkin' of
that pesky fork. So to-day I was boun' I'd get
my dinner; so I cuts it up an' spoon-victuals it,
for fear of hurtin' the feelin's of the best payin'
boarder. City ways is uncommon troublesome,
when ye ain't let eat the way is most handy. But
I don't care if I go to the theayter with ye. I
never see the inside of one of them places."

"Oh, a real theatre is nothing like the dining-
rooms of the hotels, where you saw the amateur

theatricals," said the posted Norman; "and father wouldn't let us go if it were any harm. He said we could take you, captain."

" No; an' I reckon the governor wouldn't be for goin' to no place he shouldn't go," said the captain reflectively. " An' he was along of you t'other night, wasn't he?"

Norman and Douglas, anxious to overcome any scruples the old man might have, assured him that uncle Rutherford went quite often to the " theayter," and thus quieted any remaining qualms of conscience which he might have; for Captain Yorke pinned his faith on uncle Rutherford, and all that the governor did was right in his eyes. So the expedition to the theatre was arranged to the satisfaction of my brothers, who anticipated much amusement in watching the impression the play would make upon the unsophisticated old veteran.

But a shock was in store for them which they had not foreseen; for the amount of observation which the captain saw fit to draw upon the party was almost too much for even their well-seasoned boyish nerves.

For the sake of obtaining an uninterrupted view of the stage, the boys had secured seats which the event proved to be too conspicuous for their comfort. No sooner were they all seated than the captain began with his comments and criticisms, his " them's my opinions," in a manner and tone

which they vainly strove to moderate. Fortunately
they were in the main complimentary and approving ; and the old seaman's quaint appearance, his
evidently childlike ignorance and inexperience,
diverted those of the audience who were within
hearing, and led them to be indulgent to his rather
obtrusive reflections upon men and things.

"Wal," he said, gazing around and above him,
up at the lofty frescoed ceiling, the sparkling
crystal chandelier, the rich curtains, and other
adornments of the house, — "wal, it does beat all !
It goes ahead of any meetin'-house I ever see ;
an', I say, 'tain't fair on the Almighty to be
makin' a better place for to be pleasurin' in, than
what we makes for him to be praised in. Yes,
sir ; an' them's my opinions, an' I stands by 'em.
What's them folks up in them little cubby-holes
fur ?" pointing to the boxes. "Oh," as Douglas
explained, " they's high an' mighty, be they ? can't
set along of the multitude ? Wal, every man, an'
woman too, to her own likin' ; I'd as lief be here.
Seems kinder conspicuous like, settin' up thar, an'
whiles I ain't ashamed to show my face afore no
man, I don't hanker after settin' up to be stared
at."

Happily the occupants of the boxes were beyond
the reach of his voice, or at least of the tenor of
his remarks ; but the boys were on tenterhooks
lest their garrulous companion should give offence.
But from the moment that the curtain went up,

and the mimic scene presented itself to his gaze, he sat spell-bound and silent, perfectly absorbed in the vivid portrayal of the chief character in the drama.

The great actor appeared first in the rôle of a celebrated man of his own profession, an actor of bygone days, whose name will always be famous; and from the moment that he stepped upon the stage, it was all reality to Captain Yorke. There was no "pretendin' he was other folks," to him, as it had been when he had witnessed the amateur theatricals and tableaux at the Point; and with a hand upon either knee, he leaned eagerly forward, his eyes fixed upon the scene before him, and absolutely speechless in his breathless interest. But when the curtain came down after the first act, he broke forth again to the edification and delight of those within hearing. Ladies listened and smiled at the simple-hearted old man; and gentlemen, who were near enough, encouraged him to ramble on, evidently considering him a novel species of entertainment, second only to that which was passing upon the stage. He was a character as good as any there.

Norman, enchanted with the sensation his charge was making, would put no check upon him; but the more shrinking Douglas was not so well pleased. Still, seeing that no offence was given, but rather the contrary, he possessed his soul in patience, devoutly wishing, however, that it was time for the close of the performance, which, under these circumstances, afforded him no pleasure. And as the captain's excitement grew with each succeeding act, and the encouragement of those about him, and he grew more and more superior to considerations of time and place, Douglas would fain have quitted his seat and the theatre; and was only restrained from doing so, because he thought it would be mean to leave Norman in the lurch.

At length came the farce "Dundreary Married;" and the captain, who, it afterwards appeared, had in former years suffered divers things at the hand of an obnoxious mother-in-law, grew more excited than ever, and became furiously indignant, not only at the all-assuming lady, but also at the supine Dundreary, who allowed himself to be thus imposed upon. He grumbled and muttered, and really seemed as if he would make for the stage, as he said, "to give the old creetur a piece of his mind." Even Norman was now uneasy lest he should make more demonstration than was meet, while Douglas did his best to induce both his companions to come out; but the captain was immovable, and not to be persuaded. Indeed, he scarcely seemed to heed Douglas's arguments, so intent was he on the fortunes of the persecuted husband. His delight when that hero showed symptoms of some spirit was unbounded; and when at last he roused himself altogether from the *laisser aller* which had suffered so long and patiently, and fairly bade the lady leave his house and his wife to his own authority and protection, the old man sprang to his feet, and, waving his hat in the air, exclaimed in a voice which rang in stentorian tones through the house, —

"Pitch into her, my lad! Give it to her! That's right. Pitch into the mother-in-law!"

The effect, as may be imagined, was electric. There was a moment's pause, then a laugh; then, as Norman and Douglas fairly dragged and hustled the captain into his seat, the inimitable actor bowed and waved his hand to the old man, who had, as it were, paid such an involuntary tribute to his powers; and the next moment a storm of applause broke forth, in compliment to both, it would appear, — to the gratified actor, who had thrown his spell over the guileless old sailor to such an extent as to render him insensible to aught else, and to the innocent spectator who had been thus impressed by his matchless impersonations. As the performance came to a close, and the audience were leaving the house, the captain the centre of all eyes around him, an usher made his way to him, bearing a request from the star that he would step behind the scenes and shake hands with him.

Nothing loath, the captain readily consented, inviting the boys to go with him; but this Douglas, much disturbed by the notoriety of the evening, flatly refused, while bold Norman, who had no fear of man before his eyes, agreed to accompany him. Indeed, it was not safe to lose sight of him ; there was no knowing of what vagaries the captain might be guilty if he were left entirely to his own devices. Norman felt that he was capable of any thing, and that he must keep a secure hold upon him. Moreover, the old man was not at all familiar with the city streets, and he must be guided safely to his boarding-house.

When they arrived behind the scenes, the great actor shook hands heartily with the old seaman, thanking him for the tribute which he had paid him. But here the captain's enthusiasm fell flat. Meeting the object of his sympathy face to face, and as man to man, and finding that the interesting scenes he had just witnessed were but an inimitable mimicry, was a great disappointment ; and he seemed to feel wronged and defrauded in some way.

"There warn't nothin' real about it," he said indignantly and in a hurt tone to the boys, as they took their way homeward. "There warn't nothin' true at all. There bean't no mother-in-law, nor wife, nor nothin' ; there warn't even any chap with the long whiskers, for it warn't hisself at all, though he said it was — that t'other one shook han's with me, and said I'd give him a big compliment. 'Twas all purtendin' an' makin' b'lieve. It's a shame an' a sin for to go makin' out so life-like ye are what ye ain't, an' takin' folks in so. It's kinder cheatin' play, *I* think ; an' Mis' Yorke, she wurn't jes' so easy in her min' 'bout me goin' to the theayter, an' I reckon I've come to her way of thinkin' ; an' thank ye kindly, boys, but there'll be no more theayter-goin' fur me. The Scriptur says, ' A fool an' his money is soon parted,' an' — meanin' no ungratefulness to you, boys — I've faith to b'lieve it ; for it's not good manners, neither good deeds, to make out that way, an' take folks in. An' them's my opinions, an' I'll stan' by 'em ! "

The last thing the boys heard, as the door of his temporary home closed upon him, was, "No more theayters for me ; they're clean agin' Scriptur."

This, of course, was great fun for our frolicsome Norman, always ready for a joke or a good story ; and although Douglas had not taken unalloyed pleasure in the events of the evening, he, too, could see the droll side of them now that they were over. They were rehearsed with great glee at the breakfast-table the next morning ; and it occurred to me that here, if he chose to use it, was the opportunity for Jim to revenge himself for some of the sneers cast upon him by Theodore Yorke. I was wicked enough, however, not to suggest the idea to any one else, lest a word of warning or counsel should restrain him ; and in the sequel Jim proved himself far the better Christian of the two, in spite of the superior advantages which had always been mine.

This happened to be Friday, when he brought home from school his weekly report, which he always took at once to Milly. The record for this week proved an unusually favorable one; but he had more to add to this.

"Miss Milly," he said, after she had expressed her pleasure at the progress he was making and at his standing in "conduct," — "Miss Milly, I was real forgivin' an' like livin' up to the mark you sot us for doin' unto others, in school to-day. But it does come awful hard, when you get the chance to pay off a feller, to let it slip; an' I don't know as I could have done it if it hadn't been for thinkin' of the old captain himself, an' how good he'd been to me, an' that I wouldn't like to go back on *him.*"

Light flashed upon Milly. The boy had been tempted to make use of the occurrences of the preceding evening to revenge himself upon Theodore Yorke for his previous slights and insults; and had refrained, chiefly from loyalty to his old friend, it is true, but, perhaps, partly prompted by the wish to do right.

It had so happened, that two boys in the class had been at the theatre also, and had been witnesses of the captain's antics, but without knowing who he was, or of his connection with Theodore. In recess they told the story, doubtless with more or less of exaggeration, of the old countryman who had made himself so conspicuous and — according to their showing — so ridiculous at last night's entertainment.

Of course Jim at once recognized the hero of the tale; but not so Theodore, his grandfather having, for a wonder, preserved a discreet silence on the subject, being totally unaware that he had exhibited himself in an unusual way on the occasion. Perhaps the poor captain had felt a little mortified that he had been so carried away by that which was, after all, "on'y pretendin'," and did not care to rehearse his experience.

However that may be, Theodore had heard nothing of it, and laughed and jeered with the other boys at the more than graphic relation of his two schoolmates.

Strong was the temptation to Jim to expose him, and to draw upon his enemy the laugh which must follow; but, to his credit be it said, he refrained, except in so far as to give him a knowing look which conveyed to that amiable youth the conviction that it was no other than his grandfather who was furnishing food for merriment to half the school, and that Jim was aware of it and held this rod over him. The knowledge that this was so was not calculated to soften Theodore's animosity toward Jim. Disposed as he was to raise a laugh or a sneer at the expense of another, he

could not endure them himself; and to feel that he
was thus in the power of the boy whom he hated,
was intolerable to him.   From this time, however,
it gave him a wholesome awe of Jim, and proved
a check upon him; and "Jim Grant Garfield
Rutherford Livingstone Washington" rang less
often over the playground, now that he ceased to
lead in the cry upon the claimant of so many
names.

CHAPTER IX.

MATTY.

MATTY.

"Amy, what are you pondering?"

"Men and things in general and their iniquities in particular; my own not being included, they being nothing worth speaking of," I answered, rather evasively, not being disposed at present to make public the nature of my cogitations, which really had to do with my own shortcomings.

"We will pass over the modesty of the remark," said Bessie Sanford, "but we insist upon knowing — do we not, Milly? — the tenor of the meditations which have actually kept you quiet for — let me see — I think it must be full two minutes by the clock."

"That inquisitive spirit of yours needs repression, Elizabeth," I said: "therefore I shall not yield to your demands,"

"Then bid farewell to peace," was the rejoinder. And knowing Elizabeth Sanford well, I meditated a precipitate flight; but she divined my intention, and, seizing upon me, held me prisoner, and made good her threat until I succumbed, first freeing my mind of my opinion as to the conduct of my captor.

"Never mind. We will leave the results of that case to the future," she said ; "the present question has only to do with yourself, and the unburdening of your secrets. Your inward communings are of such rare occurrence, that when you do indulge in them, your friends are entitled to benefit by them. — Is it not so, Milly?"

"Reap what benefit you may, then," I answered. "I was thinking how I was going to waste."

"H'm'm," said Bessie, releasing her grasp upon my shoulders, and gazing with an air of deep meditation out of the window near which we sat. "Fred Winston would doubtless feel complimented by that sage conclusion ; but if you feel so decidedly that you are throwing yourself away, it is not yet too late for you to draw back, and" —

"Your remarks are too frivolous to bear the consideration of a well-balanced mind, Elizabeth," I interrupted, "and therefore I decline to notice them further than to say that you are entirely wide of the mark. Perhaps I did not express myself in language as choice as I might have used ; but what I meant to say was — to quote the copy-books — that 'opportunities imply obligations,' and that, while my opportunities are many, the obligations arising therefrom have *not* been fulfilled."

I had spoken jokingly, almost mockingly, nevertheless I really meant what I said ; but any thing like a sober reflection or solemn view of life's duties was so new from me, that for a moment my sister and friend were struck dumb with astonishment.

Then Bessie gave vent to a smothered groan.

" Listen to the words of wisdom !" she ejaculated. "The depth of her! And whence and since when, may I inquire, arises thus suddenly so solemn a view of your responsibilities? They are not wont to weigh upon your mind."

"That is just it," I said. "I am in earnest, not in joke, whatever you may think. It has, rather suddenly I allow, dawned upon me, that I am a perfectly useless member of society; or rather, the conviction has been forced upon me by the words of Allie, whom I overheard informing Daisy that I was very nice and lovely, but the *uselessest* person in the house. Loyal Daisy was indignant, and questioned the justice of the remark; but it opened up a field of reflection to me, and I am obliged to admit its truth. Since I left school last spring, what have I done but amuse myself, and attend readings and lectures, which amounts to the same thing, as the motive is purely selfish?"

" You have made 'food for the gods,'" said Bessie demurely.

I turned upon her.

" For that remark you shall have cause to regret that you ever were born," I retorted, "and I would not have believed it of you, Bessie. But seriously, girls, I am longing for an object in life on which

I can expend some of the capabilities of which I feel myself possessed."

"I thought you had been supplied with one since the 15th of last November," said Bessie, "but " —

"Will you leave that subject out of the question?" I again interrupted. "If not, there will be trouble between the houses of Sanford and Livingstone."

"Why can't you two be what Daisy calls 'common-sensible,' and tell what is at the bottom of all this?" said Milly, joining for the first time in the conversation.

"I am sure that I am showing an unusual amount of common-sense," I rejoined, "for I have in all seriousness just awakened to a sense of my shortcomings towards humanity in general, and am longing for an object on which to expend my superfluous energies. You, Milly, have your charges, Bill and Jim, whom you have rescued from lives of shame and crime, and who are standing monuments of the efficacy of your zeal, self-sacrifice, and good sense in their behalf (no, you need not courtesy) ; and Bessie has her old ladies to whom she so religiously devotes one afternoon in every week, no matter what temptations assail her in other directions, and who simply adore her, and for whom she does many a little kind office at divers other times. But who, outside of our family, to whose happiness I add, of course, because I am their own Amy; and — and Fred; yes, and you, dear Bessie," as a soft little reminding hand was laid upon my arm, — "who except these is any the better or happier for my existence?"

"Lots of friends and relations, you foolish child," said Bessie, while Milly dropped a re-assuring kiss upon my forehead. "What nonsense, Amy! I do not know any one who is a more general favorite."

"Well, allowing that it is so," I said, "is it not only because I am merry and full of life, and make things a little cheerful around me? Point to one thing useful or of real lasting benefit that I have ever done, and I will thank you. I have loved Aunt Emily's hospital cottage by the sea, for her sake and for dear little Amy's, and have worked a little for that; but it has been a real pleasure and enjoyment to me, and has never involved one moment's self-sacrifice."

Modesty will not allow me to put down here all that Milly and Bessie in their partial affection said to persuade me that I was not altogether a useless member of society at large. Delightful as it was to hear, it did not succeed in quieting my newly awakened conscience or sense of responsibility; and perhaps Milly on her part did not intend that it should do so.

"She evidently must be furnished with an *object*," said Bessie; "nothing else will satisfy her;

and as she seems to have something of the feeling
of the monks and nuns of old, that the more disagreeable the duty the greater the credit, let us
satisfy her by finding her a most unpleasant one.
Oh, charming ! I have thought of just the thing. —
Why not adopt as your particular charge, Amy,
that most unattractive young cripple, Matty Blair?
She will probably satisfy all your longings for self-
sacrifice, in a way which can leave nothing to be
desired."

"The very thing," I answered, delighted to
have found so soon an "object" on which to
expend the benevolent yearnings with which I
had been seized, — not so suddenly as Milly and
Bessie believed; for, for some time past, I had had
a secret and rather unwelcome consciousness that
I was not doing my share toward mitigating the
general load of human misery and ignorance, — a
consciousness which Allie's words had only quick-
ened into more active life. "But, girls, I assure
you that I am not at all moved by the ascetic
notion of taking up the most disagreeable work I
can find, as a penance for former shortcomings.
I wish from my heart that Matty Blair was pretty
and straight and sweet, a typical little story-book
pauper, whom it would be a pleasure to befriend,
and who would respond amicably to my advances.
Matty, from what I know of her, will be far from
being all that ; nevertheless I shall take her up,
and see what can be done for her."

"Consult mother first, dear," said Milly. "She may see objections : they say that Matty's parents are dreadful people, and they may choose to make trouble for you. There are cases, you know, where people expect you to *pay* for being allowed to confer benefits upon them."

"I wish that we could remove the child, or both the children, entirely from the father and mother," I said.

"They will never allow that while the poor little things continue to be profitable to them," said Milly.

"You have taken up something of a task, truly," said Bessie. "First you will have those wretched parents to win over, and then that un-attractive little creature. And, Amy, although I would not wish to throw cold water upon your enthusiasm, I feel sure that your father and mother will never let you go to such a place as the home of the child must be. Milly's mission came to her, as it were, heaven-sent, it seems to me," she added in a reverent tone ; "but you must seek this out to do Matty any good, and face those dreadful relations of hers. Your father and mother will never listen to it, and they will be right. Do not try to run a tilt against wind-mills, dear."

"No, neither will I make mountains out of mole-hills," I answered lightly, although I did feel the force, yes, and the truth too, of Bessie's reasoning, and had my own doubts; "and certainly I shall not have more unpromising material to deal with than Milly had when she undertook to bring up her charges in the way they should go. Moreover, I shall not attempt to beard the lions in their den; but I suppose I have to win my way into Matty's affections or confidence, or whatever it may be that proves assailable, and if I find any way to help her, I shall ask cousin Serena to go into partnership with me. She will be protection enough anywhere, for no one could think of troubling or annoying her in any way."

"Well, I'm not so sure of that, either," said Bessie; "but I'm not going to discourage you further, and time will show. But how do you mean to set to work, Amy?"

"I do not know yet; how can I?" I answered. "I have only just thought of this, and of course I have not had time to make any plans or to think of what I shall do. I shall firstly go this very afternoon to cousin Serena; and if she thinks me, as she doubtless will, a prodigy of benevolence, self-sacrifice, and generosity, and agrees to all I ask of her, I shall attack father and mother to-night. I mean to act while the frenzy is on me, lest my ardor cool, and I see the many lions in the way which you bad girls are trying to conjure up."

Knowing myself in this respect pretty well, I was really afraid that if I gave myself too much

time for consideration of my new scheme, I might
become appalled by the difficulty and disagree-
ableness which were prophesied; and I was
determined to place myself in a position where —
unless a higher authority interfered — I could not
in pride or conscience draw back.

Milly had taken almost no part in the little
discussion between Bessie and me, generally
speaking only when she was appealed to; and I
knew by this that she did not altogether approve.
But I was a little self-willed, a state of mind not
altogether of rare occurrence with me, I am afraid;
and I chose to ignore the disapprobation which
was implied by this silence, and asked her no
questions.

And now for cousin Serena, to whom I bent
my steps at once, accompanied by Bessie, who
volunteered to go with me; though, to tell the
truth, I could have dispensed with her society for
this occasion, being afraid of the discouraging
objections and criticisms she might raise. But
she ventured none; on the contrary, she seemed
rather inclined to aid and abet me when I
broached the subject to cousin Serena, in whom
I was not disappointed. She proved herself — the
blessed soul — the most willing co-adjutor, even
more so than I desired; for, running to a closet
where she kept a bountiful provision of such
articles, she began to bring forth flannel, calico,
and stout muslin suitable to make clothes for poor

people; whereupon my spirit shrank appalled, for, if there was one occupation which I hated more than another, it was plain sewing, especially upon coarse material.

"O cousin Serena!" I said, "I am not going to sew and make clothes for Matty. It is so much easier and more convenient to buy them ready-made."

This speech, I was sorry to see, damped cousin Serena's ardor; for this working by proxy, as it were, did not at all coincide with her old-fashioned notions; and "ready-made garments" were to her a delusion and a snare, giving opportunity to Satan to find mischief for idle hands to do. I hated to disappoint her when she was so enthusiastically preparing to cut out work for both Bessie and me; but I hated still more to sew, and held my ground, being borne out by Bessie, who was not any more partial to such work than I was. Cousin Serena shook her head, and sighed over the degeneracy of the age which could content itself with other than such exquisite "hand-sewing" as she did herself.

Having gained my point, and made her promise all that I wished, I insisted that she should go home with us to dinner, taking the little bower of Dutch Johnny, the florist, by the way for a glimpse of Matty. Cousin Serena had never seen her; but I was not afraid to have her do so, unpromising object for one's charitable sympathies though she certainly was, for, the more helpless and repulsive-looking, the more would cousin Serena's tender heart warm toward her.

Our errand to Johnny's was nominally to purchase flowers, and, of course, we did invest therein, and came out bearing some of his choicest blossoms; but cousin Serena made use of the opportunity to take a close observation of Matty as she sat at her little peanut-stand in the corner, sullen and lowering, the picture of discontent and misery, as usual.

But cousin Serena did more than this; for, with the tact which she always showed in dealing with people of this class, she succeeded in arousing a slight feeling of interest in the sullen, disagreeable little cripple.

The one gift which had been granted to Matty was a profusion of beautiful hair, which, however, was never seen to perfection, as it was always braided tightly and wound in a close coil about her head, giving to the wizened, shrunken face an even older look than was natural to it. If she had any pride in any thing, it must have been in this hair, — indeed, she had little else to be proud of, — for it was always fairly tidy. Johnny, it seemed, always exacted a certain amount of cleanliness and decency as the price of her admission into his shop; not, perhaps, that he had any inherent love for this virtue, as such, or that his own comfort and happiness depended upon them, but because he feared that his trade might be injured if his customers found there such a dirty, ragged little object as Matty had formerly been. Clean hands and faces, well-brushed hair, and as much patching of ragged clothes as the neglected, worse than motherless creatures could compass, were required from Matty and Tony. His good-natured wife sometimes befriended them in this way, and put in a few stitches for them ; the result being profitable in more ways than one. It was she, and not the miserable, intemperate mother, who plaited Matty's glossy locks in the heavy braid which she then wound round her head.

Cousin Serena went up to the peanut-stand, invested in Matty's wares, the child serving her in the dull, mechanical way usual with her, and smiled kindly down at her, eliciting, however, no response.

"What pretty hair you have, Matty!" was Miss Craven's next advance ; and, as she spoke, she lightly touched with her gloved finger the shining coil which many a society belle might have envied.

A gleam lighted up the dull, heavy eyes, and Matty raised them to the dear old lady's face.

"It is almost a pity to wear it so closely bound up," continued cousin Serena ; while Bessie and I, apparently making an inspection of Johnny's stock while he was engaged with another customer, lent attentive ears to what passed, I feeling rather that my intended mission work had been taken up by other hands ; "it would show so nicely if you wore it loose and flowing as most little girls do now. I would like to see it when it is down."

With a motion marvellously quick in one so crippled, the child raised her hands, unbound the coil from about her head, and drawing her fingers through the plait, let the rippling, waving masses fall flowing over her poor, twisted, mis-shapen shoulders.

"Amy and Bessie," said cousin Serena, pursuing her advantage of playing upon the only vanity in poor Matty's nature, "Amy and Bessie, come here and see what beautiful hair this child has. It is a good deal like yours, Amy, both in color and quantity."

With another sudden motion, Matty drew the shining waves in front of her, glanced at them lovingly, and then raising her eyes to me with the first appearance of any thing like interest in them which I had ever seen, scanned my locks, and said with something of malicious triumph in her tone and look, —

"It's prettier nor her'n."

"So it is, Matty," I said, ignoring what Daisy would have called the "discompliment" to myself, and determined to strike while the iron was hot, or at least approaching an unusual degree of warmth, — "so it is; you have the very prettiest hair I ever saw."

Matty did not smile, — I never but once saw the light of a smile on her face, — but she gave a low chuckle. Evidently we had touched a chord that would respond; an ignoble one it might be, but it was something to have gained even this.

Having dismissed his customer, Johnny now came to the front.

"'Tis goot," he said, pointing to the beautiful locks; "'tis goot. Mine wife she say 'tis pest cut off dat head; bud Maddy she so moosh lofe dat head, an' 'tis so goot, I say, leaf her keep her head. So mine wife, she say, 'yes, 'tis too pad to cut dat nice head,' an' she leafs it on her, an' mine wife she comb an' prush it for Maddy. But I tells Maddy she shall sell dat head for so moosh as fife tollars if she schuse."

"Don't ye be after tellin' me mother that," said Matty, with a sudden look of angry alarm, which was really pathetic, as one gathered from it that the child felt she would no longer be allowed to keep her one cherished possession, if any idea of its pecuniary value were suggested to her mother.

"Nein, nein," answered Johnny, shaking his head and speaking with emphasis, as if to say that this was a secret he would carefully guard from the unnatural parent. "Nein, nein," he repeated. "If I tells dat mutter any tings, 'tis as dat head is so pad as is not vort notings."

"But you would not say what is not true, even

to save Matty's hair, would you?" said Miss Craven, unable to allow this more than doubtful morality to pass.

Again Johnny wagged his head, this time as one quite convinced that he was in the right, and answered: "If I tells shust one nice, leetle pit of a lie" (Johnny did not mince matters, even to his own conscience), "'tis for to keep away a great pig wrong; for if I tells dat mutter de shild's head is vort so moosh, she put dat head in de scissors de negst minit."

The kindly old Dutchman was plainly convinced that the end justified the means, and cousin Serena felt that any further discussion of the question was useless, and that it would not tend to improve Matty's moral views or those of her brother Tony, who had just come in, as both were sure to side with their friend and benefactor.

"We will hope that no one will ever touch Matty's pretty hair," she said; and I, seized with a sudden inspiration, and still appealing to Matty's vanity, said, —

"I would like to see Matty's hair flowing over a dark-blue dress. How it would set it off! Would you like a blue dress, Matty? Your hair will look so pretty over it if you wear it down."

Matty looked rather askance at me. She evidently regarded me as a rival in the matter of hair, and was not inclined to accept any advances on my part; but friendly, jolly little Tony answered for her; while she hesitated, evidently meditating some ungracious answer.

"Oh, wouldn't she though, miss! I guess she would like it, an' her hair would look awful pooty on it, an' when we goes to the Sunday-school festival, — when it's Easter, ye know, — Matty'll wear the blue dress, an' her hair down on it, an' she'll look as good as any of the girls there, an' better, 'cause there isn't one of 'em has hair like Matty's. — An' I'll tell ye, Matty, if the lady, — she's one of Jim's young ladies, — if she gives ye the blue dress, we'll keep it to Mrs. Petersen's if she'll let us, so ma can't get it for the drink. — Are ye goin' to give it to her, miss?"

"Indeed I am," I answered to the eager question. "Come now, Matty, stand up, and we'll measure you for the dress. Perhaps I can find one ready-made, and you shall have it to-morrow. — Johnny, can you lend me a yard-measure?"

Johnny produced one; and Matty, still half doubtful whether or no to be gracious, and eying me with a gaze which had some lingering viciousness in it, rose half reluctantly to her feet. Standing so, her deformity was even more visible than it was when she was seated; and it took all my nerve and power of will to take the measure of the mis-shapen shoulders without shrinking from the touch. And then I saw the improbability, I might say the impossibility, of finding in any ready-made-clothing store, a dress which would fit the

twisted form.   One must be made on purpose ; one
which would set at defiance all rules of symmetry ;
and how to have it completed to-morrow, even late
in the day to-morrow ?   Where should I go to have
such an order filled by the time I desired it ?   And
I believed from what I had seen of Matty that the
non-fulfilment or postponement of my hasty, ill-
considered promise would be enough to excite all
her enmity again.   However, I said nothing until
we were out of the little shop, when I exclaimed at
my own want of fore-thought, and asked where I
could go to have my order fulfilled without delay.

"You can't do it," said Bessie.   "Even at the
stores where they profess to furnish costumes at
twenty-four hours' notice, they would not agree to
give you, in so short a time, a dress for which they
can use no ordinary pattern.   Amy," — with what
seemed to be a most irrelevant change of subject,
— "is any one coming to your house to dinner
to-night ?"

"Cousin Serena, and yourself if you will," I
answered.

"Yes, I intended to suggest that you should
invite me," answered Bessie, "and, had you proved
obdurate, should have appealed to Milly or your
mother.   Well, there will be four of us : yourself,
cousin Serena, Milly, and myself ; and we will press
the mother and Mrs. Rutherford into the service.
Let us go to Arnold's, buy some suitable material,
—and we all know what cousin Serena is with

scissors and thimble, — coax her to cut out a dress for Matty, and we will all devote the evening, perhaps the whole night, to it. By our united exertions, I think that we can surely accomplish it in time for you to take it to her to-morrow, and your credit will be saved."

" If we were not in the street, I should fall upon you with kisses and tears of gratitude," I answered ecstatically ; "as it is, consider yourself embraced. — Cousin Serena, will you help us ?"

There was no question of that : cousin Serena was only too glad to give us her services ; and although, as I have said, she needed to be guided and tyrannized over in the matter of style and fashion where her own dress was concerned, she was an expert in fashioning garments for the poor.

Bessie's idea was acted upon forthwith. We took our way down to Arnold's, purchased the necessary material, and, lest it should not be sent home in time, bid pride hide its head, and carried the parcels ourselves.

Jim beamed upon us when he gathered, from the conversation around the dinner-table, to what the evening was to be devoted, and became quite an overpowering nuisance with his pressing attentions to the young ladies.

The dress was so nearly completed that night that Milly and I had but little difficulty in finishing it for the next afternoon.

Father and mother gave consent to my pursuing

my benevolent intentions with regard to Matty, so far as I could do it without venturing into the abode of her wretched parents, but positively forbade my going there even under the guidance and protection of cousin Serena. Indeed, the fear of them which Tony and Matty showed augured little good or encouragement for those who would benefit these children, unless some profit therefrom, was to accrue to the elder Blairs themselves.

The dress was ready in good time, and supplemented by the addition of a warm sack of the same color from mother and a little cloth cap from aunt Emily. A hood had been in the thoughts of the latter, as warmer and more suitable ; but I had begged for the cap as affording better opportunity for the display of Matty's hair. "Poor little object !" I pleaded : "why not allow her the gratification of this small vanity?" and aunt Emily yielded, as she was sure to do when any one's small whims and fancies were to be satisfied.

Maria made the garments into a neat parcel for me ; and I, thinking to give Jim a pleasure, summoned him on his return from school to be the bearer thereof, and to accompany me to Johnny's. That Jim was pleased, was an assured fact ; and his tongue wagged incessantly though respectfully all the way until we arrived at our destination. Then while I opened the parcel, and presented Matty with the dress and other articles, he stood by in delighted contemplation, looking from me to Matty as if he would say to her, "This is my young mistress;" to me, "This is my *protégée.*"

As for Matty, she appeared, so far as she showed any feeling at all, to consider that the gifts were altogether due to him; and she vouchsafed no word of thanks to me. Not that I cared for expressions of gratitude; but I felt a little hopeless as I saw how entirely I had failed to make any impression on her.

Tony, however, who was present again, was profuse in his thanks, and really seemed to feel all that he said.

The shining hair fell like a shielding veil over Matty's deformity again to-day; and after this it became her practice to wear it so when she was away from home. There she wore it tightly bound up, and kept it as much out of sight as possible; fearing, poor little creature, that she might be bereft of it, should any idea of its pecuniary value enter her mother's mind.

CHAPTER X.

A COLD BATH.

A COLD BATH.

"WELL, Jim," I said, as I returned home in the fast-gathering twilight, with my escort trotting beside me, "how are you getting on now at school? I have not heard lately."

"I'm havin' an awful hard time just now, Miss Amy," he answered, coming nearer, — "an awful hard time."

"How is that?" I asked. "Are they pressing you too much? Have they given you too many lessons, or are those you had before becoming harder?"

"Neither, miss," he answered. "'Tain't the lessons; I don't mind them. Lessons ain't nothin' — I mean lessons ain't any thing" — Jim was growing more choice in language, and taking infinite pains with his parts of speech — "when a feller has such good help as Miss Milly or Mr. Edward. If they're too hard for me, one of 'em always helps me an' makes 'em plain, an' I keep along good enough in the classes. But it's the keepin' cool, an' not flyin' out when I get provoked, 'specially with that Theodore Yorke. Miss

Amy, you never saw the like of him. He's just the meanest chap ever breathed ; and the way he finds out things you don't want him to know, an' keeps bringin' 'em up an' naggin' about 'em, is the worst."

"All the more credit to you, then, Jim, if you keep your temper under such provocation," I answered soothingly, "and you show yourself by far the better man of the two. You know the Bible says, 'Greater is he that ruleth his spirit than he that taketh a city.'"

"Well, Miss Amy," he said, "I guess it ain't no such rememberin' nor Bible texes that keeps me cool. It's lots of other things. First, I do want awful bad to do credit to Miss Milly ; then I don't want to fight Theodore, nor have a real sharp fallin' out, on account of the captain an' Mrs. Yorke ; then I'm thinkin', if I don't learn to hold my temper now, how will it be if I come to be President of these States ? I s'pose there's lots of things that'll be provokin', an' hard to stand, when you're President ; and if Congress don't want to mind you right spang off when you tell 'em to do a thing, an' goes to foolin' round about it, I s'pose it don't do to be flyin' out, 'cause then folks would think you wasn't fit to be President. Besides, when one's mad he can't think about the best way to do things, an' I might make foolish laws they wouldn't like. But most of all it will be a great deal better way to get even with Theodore if I come out first with Mr." —

Here he suddenly checked himself, and even in the dim twilight I could see the color mounting to the roots of his carroty hair. He had evidently been on the verge of some disclosure which he would have regretted, and no questions succeeded in drawing forth any thing further from him.

He had been sufficiently candid, however, in admitting that he was not influenced, in the struggle with himself, by any abstract notions of right and wrong, or by any special desire to please a higher power. But that he had some motive still undeclared, and of greater weight with him than any of those he had mentioned, I was convinced; and why should he wish to keep it back?

However, my cogitations on the subject, and Jim's confidences, were now cut short by the appearance at the corner, of another escort, who took charge of me at once with a very decided remonstrance against my remaining out till this hour "with only the protection of that boy."

This was a slight which would have wounded Jim to the quick had he heard it, which he fortunately did not, as it was spoken in an undertone; and he was evidently pleased to be freed from an attendance which had become embarrassing to him by his own indiscretion.

"What do you suppose he could have meant?" I asked of Milly that night, after I had rehearsed to her, in the privacy of our own room, my conversation with Jim.

"I am sure I do not know," said my sister. "If it were possible, I should think he meant uncle Rutherford's prize; but as he does not and can not know of that, of course it cannot be. And while we must all wish that he were acting from a higher motive than any of these, still it is a great point gained, that he is so learning to control himself; the habit will be formed, and he will learn to be his own master. But I fear that Theodore Yorke is not a truthful or upright boy. Even our own boys, who see so little of him, call him a sneak; and although he has a bold, self-assertive manner, it has none of Jim's frankness. Oh, uncle Rutherford, I wish that you could have seen things differently!"

But as uncle Rutherford had not only seen things in his own light, but had acted thereon, there was nothing for us to do beyond giving Jim what help we could. There was little, however, a lady could do to help a boy in a public school in his struggle with adverse circumstances, save by advice and encouragement; and Milly did not fail him in these.

Taking a hint from what I had seen of Jim's influence over Matty, I now based my plans for her benefit and regeneration upon that, in addition to the play upon her vanity by means of that wonderful and much-prized hair. Jim, too, I knew would paint me and all my doings in glowing colors, making much of any little kindness I might do for her.

The blue dress and other decent clothes were kept at kind Mrs. Petersen's "for fear of the drink," and Matty donned them there when she found occasion to wear them ; and this led me to carry out the idea of rescuing the children, Matty and Tony, entirely from the intemperate wretches who dishonored the names of father and mother, and placing them under the care of Mrs. Petersen. So long as the two little cripples brought home such portion of their weekly earnings as Jim had agreed should be allowed to Blair and his wife, the latter cared little where or how the neglected children spent their time, especially as they were now provided with their dinner as a part of the price of their services at the peanut-stand.

The disapprobation in Milly's manner, which I had noticed and wondered at, when my new enterprise was under consideration, had altogether vanished after that first afternoon ; and she had not only helped with all her might in the making of the blue dress, but she had ever since been interested and full of thoughtful suggestion.

"Milly," I said to her one day soon after, "why did you seem so unwilling to have me undertake to care for that little cripple ? You surely had formed a precedent for such things in our family. I never could understand your objections; for, that you had objections, I could not help seeing."

Milly laughed.

"I find that such objections as I entertained were not well founded," she answered.

"Perhaps so, but that does not tell me what they were," I insisted.

"Well," she said, "I was a little afraid that Jim might feel that you were trespassing on his preserves; and your field for charity is so large, and his so small, that I did not wish him to imagine that he was interfered with."

"Well, that is disposed of, for he is delighted with my co-operation," I said. "Now, what else was it?"

Milly was reluctant to say; but I persisted, and at last she answered, —

"I feared that it was only — that you would soon tire of it, Amy, and that the experiment would then prove good neither for you nor for Matty; but in that too I hope I was wrong."

After events left no room to prove whether or no I should have been long steadfast to my purpose of caring for poor Matty; that was taken out of my hands.

Jim's report from school had been one of unbroken credit for weeks now, — in conduct, that is; and to those who knew the boy's fiery, impulsive, and, until he fell under Milly's care, untrained, nature, the record was a remarkable one. In his classes, he was doing fairly well, and making progress of which he had no need to be ashamed, but his lessons were by no means always perfect ; and, happily, it was not so much to them that we looked, as the chief means for his gaining uncle Rutherford's prize, for Theodore's standing in this respect was generally a better one than his own.

I had noticed, and Milly at length came to do so, that if the record was an unusually good one, and he received an extra amount of praise, he still always appeared sheepish and ill at ease, and as though he had something on his mind which he was half-inclined to make known. But he never came to the point of doing so, and Milly had ceased to ask him.

We were kept pretty well informed, too, of the progress and standing of Theodore Yorke; partly by uncle Rutherford's interest in the matter and the inquiries he made of the teachers every week, and also by the captain's pride in his grandson, whom he considered a prodigy of learning. The boy was certainly bright and clever, as was Jim; and the two kept fairly even in their record, both for lessons and conduct.

But while Jim continued to grow in popularity with both teachers and scholars, it was not so with Theodore, and there was a strong prejudice against him, especially among the boys. There seemed to be no particular cause of offence or instance of wrong-doing to be brought against him, but there it was; and neither masters nor schoolmates seemed to place any confidence in him.

As far as trade went, Jim was certainly making a good thing out of the school; for, owing to his persuasions, to say nothing of that leaning toward peanuts which is a marked feature of every boyish mind, the calls at Matty's stand on the way to and from the school were very frequent; and while pennies and nickels flowed in upon the small vender, peanut-shells were scattered all over the building and playground, until at last they called forth a remonstrance from the janitor. Finding this of no avail, he threatened an appeal to the higher authorities; but, as he was a good-natured old soul, he hesitated to draw reproof upon the boys, when about this time an incident occurred which made complaint unnecessary, as peanuts became prohibited altogether within school bounds.

"Jim," said a boy, coming to him one morning before the school-bell rang, "do you see the lot of peanuts Theodore Yorke has?"

"I don't pay much heed to Theodore Yorke or his havin's," answered Jim scornfully. "It's no odds to me if he has bushels of peanuts or nary a one."

"But maybe it is odds to you," answered the other boy. "I ain't a telltale; but Theodore Yorke's always buyin' peanuts off of your stand, an' you can bet he comes away from that stand

with a lot more peanuts for two cents or five cents
than any one of the rest of us does."

Jim turned sharply upon him.

"You don't mean Matty gives him over measure,
Rob?" he said.

"She don't *give* him over measure, but he gets
over measure," replied Rob; "an' I tell you 'cause
I think it's a shame to be cheatin' you an' the
girl."

"What is it, then? Out with it!" exclaimed
Jim. "I can see how she can cheat him givin'
him short measure if she likes, but I can't see
how he can cheat her gettin' *over* measure."

"S'pose when she's measurin' out what he's
asked for, he puts his hand into the big basket
on her other side, maybe more than once, too;
how'll that do for helping himself to long measure,
hey?" said Robert.

"How do you know?" asked Jim, trying to
control his rising fury until he had all the facts.

"I've seen him do it more than once, an' more
than twice," replied Rob. "You know we live in
the same house, and mostly come on to school
together, an' both him an' me is apt to stop for
peanuts. And the first time I saw him do that,
taking out a handful extra for himself, was one
morning when I hadn't any money to buy; but
he stopped in, and I staid out, 'cause it was too
kind of tantalizing to go in and smell 'em all
freshly roasted, and not get any; and I was look-

ing in between the posies and plants in the shop,
and when Matty was filling up her measure for him
— only the two-center one — I saw him do that
mean trick; on a girl, too, and she a hunchback!
He slipped his hand into the basket, and carried it
full to his dinner-basket. So after that I watched,
whether I went in or staid out; and he never
lets a time go by that he don't hook a handful,
maybe two, if he gets the chance. You see, that
girl's got such a lot of thick hair hanging round
her, it's most like a thick veil, and would keep
her from seeing what goes on behind or by the
side of her. I tell you, Jim, I guess with one
time and another he must have bagged two or
three quarts of peanuts off of you and the hunchback, and I couldn't let it go on any longer. This
very morning he bought two cents worth, and
hooked as much as five."

Jim's indignation had grown higher and fiercer
with every succeeding word of this story; and,
unfortunately, at this moment Theodore came
around a corner of the school-building upon the
playground, and, as a combination of ill luck
would have it, he was eating peanuts, which he
extracted from a pocket whose bulging proportions showed that the stock from which he was
drawing was a large one.

The sight inflamed Jim's passion beyond all
bounds; and he immediately advanced upon
Theodore in a manner and with a look which left

no doubt as to his purpose. The culprit dodged
the first blow aimed at him; but in another instant
Jim's hand was upon his collar, while, with language which was neither choice nor mild, he
struck him several times, and would have continued the blows had he not in his turn been
seized upon by one of the masters, who had seen
the whole thing, to whom it appeared to be the
most unprovoked attack.

Jim's fury had so passed beyond restraint, that for
a moment neither the sight of the teacher nor his
stern voice calling him to order had the effect of
bringing him to his senses; and he even turned
upon the gentleman himself, probably believing
for the moment that it was one of the other boys.
His crestfallen, mortified look when he was recalled to himself did not help him in the estimation of the teacher, who took it as a sign of
guilt; while Theodore, once freed from his assail-
ant, stood by as the martyr and peaceable boy
who would not strike a blow, even in self-defence.
Rob, meanwhile, frightened by the consequences
of his disclosures to Jim, slunk off without waiting
to bear testimony to the provocation which Jim
believed himself to have received.

Jim was "reported," of course, and punished;
and the knowledge that this must come to the
ears of Miss Milly and Mr. Rutherford did not
tend to soothe his anger, nor did he feel that his
desire for vengeance was yet satisfied. As he

had been deprived of his recess, however, he had no immediate opportunity of gratifying it; and when school was over, the principal, who was a just though strict man, and who was particularly interested in uncle Rutherford's scheme and the two rivals for his prize, called both Jim and Theodore before him, and inquired into the cause of the disturbance.

Now, Theodore was perfectly well aware of this, for Jim had not failed to make use of his tongue as well as his fists, and he knew that in some way his petty and oft-repeated thefts had come to light; but he was not going to confess his own iniquities, and Jim was what Rob Stevens, with less reason, had asserted himself to be, — "no telltale."

He rather sulkily replied, to the questions of the principal, that "Theodore knew, and could tell if he liked;" but Theodore doggedly declared that he had given and knew of no cause of offence, and that the attack had been entirely without reason.

As Jim could not be persuaded to bring any accusation other than the scornful, ferocious looks with which he regarded Theodore; while Theodore himself was evidently uneasy and fearful lest his antagonist should speak the truth, — Mr. Rollins was convinced that the latter was really, in some way, to blame. But of course he could not punish him without reason; while Jim had been caught red-handed, and must, at least, be reprimanded and warned. The gentleman told him that he forfeited his recess for a week, and that, if he trespassed again in this manner, he would be degraded to a lower class.

Jim received his sentence in silence; but when Mr. Rollins spoke of the penalty to follow future offending, his ruddy face blanched. *That* meant not only disgrace in the school, but, what was far worse to him, before Miss Milly and Mr. Rutherford, and the lessening of his "chance" with the latter, and Theodore's preferment above him.

As the boys were dismissed from the tribunal of justice, and turned away, Mr. Rollins caught a glance of gratified malice which Theodore cast at the other boy; and he was more than ever persuaded that there was something behind all this, and that Theodore was, perhaps, the one who was the most to blame.

They had reached the door, when Jim turned, and, coming back to the desk of the principal, said in a low tone, "Thank you, sir, for not puttin' any thing more on me than the recess. I don't mind that so much, an' I'll try hard not to break rules again; but *you* can't tell how hard it is not to get mad when the mad lies so near the top, an' you're gettin'" — "cheated" would have been the next word, but Jim checked himself ere it was spoken.

"Do I not, my boy?" answered the gentleman: then seeing that Theodore was lingering at the door as if anxious to hear what passed, he said to him, with something of sternness in his voice, born of the doubt as to which of the two boys was the greater culprit, "Go on, sir, you have no need to wait;" adding to himself, "That boy has a guilty conscience." Then, when Theodore had closed the door behind him, he turned again to Jim, and continued, "You are mistaken, Jim, if you think I do not know what it is to struggle with a quick temper."

"You, sir?" said Jim.

"Yes, I," answered Mr. Rollins; and then he followed with the story of his own struggles with a passionate temper, and the final victory over himself, with much good advice and encouragement to Jim. Encouraged the boy certainly did feel, as he left the presence of the master, fortified with new resolutions for the future.

But master Theodore was not to escape without his share of punishment.

As his own ill luck would have it,—perhaps it would be better to say, as a righteous retribution would have it,—as he was on his way home from school, and was crossing the park on which our house fronted, he fell in with three or four of his classmates, among them Rob Stevens, the witness of his thefts.

"What have you done with Jim?" asked one of the boys.

"He's getting it from the commander-in-chief,"

said Theodore exultantly. "He's lost his recess for a week, and is to be put down to class four if he gets into another of his rages, as he's sure to do; and now he's taking no end of a blowing-up. The commander sent me out so I wouldn't hear it. Good enough for him. I hope he'll get it hot and heavy."

"What did *you* get?" asked Rob.

"What did I get? Nothing; why should I?" responded Theodore, who had not the slightest idea of the way by which Jim had learned of his thefts, or that here was his accuser.

"Didn't you tell why Jim pitched into you when you saw he was gettin' held up for it?" asked Rob.

"No!" roared Theodore, partly in fear, partly in anger, for he now could not fail to see that Rob knew *something*, but how much he could not tell. "I hadn't any thing to tell, and hadn't done any thing to Jim, — to his high-mightiness Jim Grant Garfield Rutherford Livingstone Washington, the fellow with a whole dictionary-full of names, and not a right to one of them but the Jim. I just wish he would get into a dozen tantrums, till he gets expelled from the school."

"Nothin' mean about you, is there?" said one of the other boys indignantly, although he was still ignorant of the cause of Jim's provocation.

But this was too much for Rob.

The boys had neared the fountain in the centre

of the park. At this season, it was never or seldom playing; but some repairs had been found necessary, and the workmen had had the jet in action for some hours, and the large basin around it was full of water. The boys stopped beside it, not noticing a tall figure which sat upon one of the park benches near.

"Nothing mean about *him!* " repeated Rob in a loud voice, which might easily be heard on the other side of the fountain, "nothing mean about Theodore Yorke! He's the meanest sneak in our school, or out of it, either! I'll tell you why Jim pitched into him. He's been stealing peanuts off of Jim's stand when the little hunchback's head was turned. I saw him, more than once, and I wasn't going to have it any longer; so I told Jim, and I'd just told him of it when Theodore came on eating peanuts, the very ones, for all I know, that I saw him steal this morning; and no wonder Jim's spirit was up, and he pitched into him. I wish he'd had it out with him, too, before Mr. Leeds came up. If he was going to be punished, he might as well be hung for a sheep as a lamb. And Jim's never said a word, I s'pose, or let on what he did it for; and you let him take all the blame. Bah! I wouldn't be you, for a cart-load of peanuts!"

"You didn't see me, either. I don't know what you're talking about!" stammered Theodore, so taken aback by the damaging testimony of this unexpected witness of his sin, that he lost all self-possession, and his looks proclaimed him guilty of the offence with which he was charged.

Uprose from the bench beyond the group the figure sitting there, and, striding towards the still unobservant boys, laid one hand upon Theodore's collar, the other on that of Rob; and the startled Theodore looked up into the stern, set face of his grandfather.

"Have I heerd aright?" said the old man in his righteous wrath. "Have I heerd my gran'son called a thief, an' a sneak, what let a boy like Jim be blamed for doin' what he had a right to do, if what this 'ere feller says is true? — Kin ye prove it?" turning to Rob, while he still kept a tight hold on either boy.

"Yes, I can," said Rob, maintaining his ground, although he was a little frightened by the captain's looks and tones; and once more he rehearsed the story in all its details.

By this time several persons, attracted by the somewhat unusual spectacle of an old man holding two boys by their collars, had stopped to hear what was going on; and there were symptoms of a crowd. Seeing this from afar, a policeman bore down upon the scene, — the very one who had had the dispute with the captain as to the propriety of Daisy playing peanut-vender on the street-corner.

As he came near, Captain Yorke released his

hold upon Rob's collar ; then tightening that upon Theodore's, the still stalwart old seaman lifted the boy from his feet, and, stepping close to the basin of the fountain, plunged him over his head in the icy water. The day had been a mild one, sunny and bright, for spring was in the air ; but the water was still sufficiently cold to make such a sudden plunge any thing but pleasant, and this summary method of punishment, well deserved though most of the spectators knew it to be, was not to be tolerated in such a public place. So thought the policeman who now came running up, as the captain, having given his grandson three good dips, lifted him dripping and shivering from the basin, and placed him upon his feet.

"What's this?" asked the officer, who had long since made his peace with the old man, who was wont to hang about the park, and in the vicinity of our house, and who amused him vastly with his comments upon men and things in the city. "What are you up to now, captain?"

"Givin' this boy a duckin' ; an' if I told ye what for, I donno but ye'd be for takin' of him up," answered the captain, disregarding all considerations of parental or family pride. "If ye fin' me a meaner one nor he is in this big town, I'll duck him, too, an' keep him under till he begs an' swears he'll mend his ways. — Now, git along home, sir," to the shaking Theodore. "I'd willin' pay for two suits of clo's to have the satisfaction of

"PLUNGED HIM OVER HIS HEAD IN THE ICY WATER."—*Page* 214.

givin' ye yer desarvins, though I don't know as ye've got 'em yet.   Git !"

Theodore, only too glad to obey, sped away like the wind ; while the captain, as the policeman was about to interfere further, turned to the officer, and, taking him by the arm, as if he were going to arrest *him*, repeated in a friendly tone, " He's had no more than his desarvin's, — young scamp ; an' them's my opinions.   I'll tell ye."

" But what are you about, ducking that boy in a public fountain ? " asked the officer, doubtful what course to pursue with the old original.   " Don't you know such a thing is a breach of the public peace ? "

" I don't know nothin' about your breaches," said the old veteran, no whit disturbed ; " but I knows I got a right to duck that boy where'er I've a min' to.   He's my gran'son, — more shame to me, — an' a little water ain't goin' to hurt him. His fam'ly's used to water, — good salt water, too," with a contemptuous look at the fluid in the fountain basin, "an' if I could wash the meanness outer him, I'd duck him a dozen times a day. Come along."

And still with his hand upon the policeman's arm, the captain turned away with him, soon satisfying the guardian of the peace that this was no case for arrest.   Barney agreed that he had the right to take the law into his own hands, although this was hardly the place for him to do so.

Of course Theodore's thefts, and the story of the grandfather's summary punishment, went the rounds of the school the next morning, and it soon reached the ears of the teachers and principal; and Theodore was called up again before the latter, this time to receive a far sterner reprimand than had been bestowed upon Jim. As the offence had been committed out of school bounds and school hours, the punishment for it did not lie within the jurisdiction of Mr. Rollins; but, in addition to that which he had received from his grandfather, it was meted out to him on the school premises. From that time he acquired the *sobriquet* of "Peanuts," — a name which, short as it was, attracted far more derision and notice than that of Jim Grant Garfield Rutherford Livingstone Washington.

And Jim, for his silence before the principal, his heroic determination to "tell no tales," was more of a favorite than ever.

Whether this tended to lessen Theodore's animosity toward him, or to soften the standing feud between them, may be judged.

The contempt and dislike which the school generally entertained for Theodore were brought to their height, when the edict was promulgated that peanuts should be no longer brought within bounds. Being a forbidden fruit, they at once acquired a value and desirableness even beyond that which they had possessed before. By some unexplained process of reasoning, the authorities had arrived at the conclusion that they were the cause of the late disturbance; and so they were tabooed, much to the displeasure of the boys, who, beside the deprivation to themselves, considered Jim a victim, as the order, of necessity, in a measure lessened his sales.

CHAPTER XI.

FIVE DOLLARS.

CHAPTER XI.

FIVE DOLLARS.

Dear old Mrs. Yorke had improved rapidly under the care of the specialist who was treating her case ; but she was ill at ease in her city quarters, partly because she was unaccustomed to her surroundings, partly because she was never certain, when the captain was away from her, that he was not doing some unheard-of thing which might bring him into a serious predicament. And now here was this trouble between Jim, of whom she and the captain were so proud and so fond, and her grandson, and the disgrace of the latter; so that just now her bed was not one of roses, and she longed for the quiet and peace of her simple seaside home.

"If Adam would but go home, and take the boy with him," she sighed to Mammy one day, "I could be easy in my mind, for I know that Jabez and Matilda Jane and Mary would look after him well, and he would be out of harm's way ; but now I wouldn't be a bit surprised if some day he turned up in the police-court, just for doin' something he thought was no harm, but that is against city rules. His ways and city folks' ways ain't alike. An' there's the boy, an' what he's done ; all the school learnin' in the world ain't goin' to pay for such a shame. No, you needn't say it was on'y a boyish trick ; you on'y say that to make me more easy like ; an' with thanks all the same to Governor Rutherford, I'd a sight rather he'd left Theodore down to the Point, an' out of the way of such temptations as he gets here. An' when they once begin that way as boys, you never know where they'll end. No, no; I wish Adam and the boy were home."

Poor Mrs. Yorke! She had, indeed, too much reason to dread the after results of "once beginning that way ;" for Theodore seemed likely to follow in the footsteps of his good-for-nothing father.

Uncle Rutherford, of course, heard of the peanut episode, and expressed a fitting censure on Theodore's conduct, both to our family and to the boy himself ; but we said among ourselves, that he not only appeared to endorse, but to enjoy, Jim's swift, passionate punishment of Theodore, and he escaped with a very slight reproof, if, indeed, the few words he said to him concerning the matter could be called reproof ; and Milly felt no fear that he had lost ground with uncle Rutherford.

Fortunately the captain, knowing little or nothing of the streets, was given, when by himself,

to haunting our neighborhood and the park opposite; so that he came much under the notice and
patronage of the friendly policeman, whose daily
beat was in that quarter, and who kept him on
many an occasion from going astray, or making a
spectacle of himself.

The captain had sought out Rob Stevens,
insisted that he should tell him just how many
times he had seen Theodore steal peanuts from
Matty, and, so far as he could judge, to what
amount each time; then counting up what he
supposed them to be worth, which he put at an
enormously high valuation — the honest old man!
— that he might be sure to err on the right side,
he forced Theodore to go with him to the stand,
and pay Matty for the stolen fruit. He endeavored, too, to make him apologize to Jim, both for
the theft of his property, and also for his contemptible meanness in keeping silent on the
occasion of Jim's attack on the playground. But
here he was powerless: Theodore absolutely and
doggedly refused to do it; and his grandfather
was obliged to content himself with relieving his
own feelings, and further expressing his sentiments on the boy's conduct, by giving him a
severe flogging.

Spring was upon us now; an early, mild, and
beautiful spring. Day after day of sunny delicious weather succeeded one another; the children came home from their walks or drives in

the Central Park, in ecstasies over the robins, blue-birds, and squirrels they had seen. In the woods at Oaklands, — whither father went once or twice a week to have an eye upon his improvements and preparations for the summer, — spring-beauties, hepaticas, and anemones, and even a few early violets, were showing their lovely faces ; and all young things — ah, and the older ones too — were rejoicing that the "winter was past and gone."

With the advent of the mild weather, Matty's stand had been removed out of doors and beneath the shelter of Johnny Petersen's shop ; and this situation proved more profitable than it had been within, as many a charitable passer-by, seeing the pitiful figure and pinched face of the poor child, would stop to purchase. During the hours of the day when the sun was warm and bright, her surroundings were not much less attractive than they had been within ; for the glass sashes of the little flower-store were generally wide open behind her, while Johnny frequently brought forth some of his plants for an airing upon the side-walk.

As his custom increased with the warm weather, and people came for potted plants and so forth for their gardens and windows, Johnny occasionally found it necessary to be away for a few hours buying new stock at the larger greenhouses and markets ; and when Mrs. Petersen did not find it convenient to take his place in the shop, he depended upon Tony to keep watch, and make small sales for him. The lame boy was bright and apt ; and Johnny had drilled him well as to prices and so forth, and found him a tolerably satisfactory substitute during his own times of absence.

One would have thought that Theodore Yorke would have avoided the neighborhood of the peanut-stand after his exposure and disgrace ; but it was not so. His grandfather had cut short the small amount of pocket-money which he had occasionally given him, and he was now left penniless, and so no more visited the place as a customer; but he seemed to take a delight in hanging around it, and annoying Matty and Tony, who were now on their guard, and watched him unceasingly. Tony and he frequently exchanged sundry compliments not suited to ears polite ; and Johnny, if he saw him, would come out and drive him away. The shop was absolutely forbidden ground to him ; within it he was not suffered to set a foot.

One bright afternoon when Johnny Petersen happened to be away, and Tony was in charge, Theodore came sauntering up to the stand, to the great dissatisfaction of the children. Matty was in her usual seat behind her table ; Tony seated on the low door-step of the store, his crutches lying on the ground beside him and within reach of his hand.

Theodore came up, glanced into the store, and, seeing that the master was absent, addressed himself to the amiable amusement of teasing and worrying those who were too helpless to defend themselves.

"Me an' Matty's lookin' out for ye, an' ye needn't come roun' to be stealin' no more pea-nuts," said Tony at length, "an' I'll call the M. P. if you comes too close to the stand. We ain't goin' to stan' no foolin', we ain't; an' Jim told us you don't have a cent of money now, so you ain't come to buy with one hand an' help yourself with t'other. It'd be helpin' yourself with both; so clear out!"

"I ain't comin' near your old peanuts," said Theodore; "an' they ain't yours, anyway."

This style of converse continued for some minutes, growing more and more personal each instant; till at last Theodore said to Matty, who, according to her usual custom, had remained perfectly silent, —

"If I had such a cushion on my back as yours, I wouldn't make it bigger piling such a heap of hair on it. You look like a barber's-shop show figger. I wonder you don't sell yourself for a show figger. You'd look so pretty an' smart."

Matty only gave him one of her most vicious looks, and clinched her small claw-like hands as though they longed to be at him; but Tony answered for her.

"They don't get no such hair to the barbers' shops without payin' lots for it," he shouted; "an' she ain't no need to make a figger of herself. She can sell it for a heap of money, — five dollars, if she chooses, — Mr. Petersen says so, an' Jim says so, too. But she ain't a-goin' to have it cut off; she likes it too much, an' the ladies likes it, Jim's ladies do, an' they telled her to leave it hang down, an' one on 'em give her a blue dress to make it look purtier on it; an' she's give her lots of things more. An' they've give me lots of things, too; the ole un she give me a whole suit for Easter, an' me an' Matty looked as good as any of 'em. An' Jim says — now you keep off," as Theodore drew nearer, "you keep off, or I'll call the M. P. He ain't so fur."

"Oh, you will, will you?" said Theodore; "you've got to catch him first, and me, too, old Hippity-hop," and with a kick he sent both crutches far beyond the reach of the lame boy, then, with a derisive laugh, ran off. And there Tony sat, helpless and unable to pursue, till a compassionate passer-by brought him the crutches; for Matty could not stoop for them. Had the old captain seen this cowardly, contemptible deed, he would probably have thought that all the waters of all the oceans could not "wash the meanness" from the soul of his grandson.

For the rest of that day and for the next, and for two or three succeeding ones, Theodore's thoughts dwelt much upon this last interview with the two cripples; but do not let it be thought, with any disquieting reproaches from his conscience, or any feeling of remorse. To him, all that had passed was a mere nothing, not worth a second thought, save for the one idea which had made a deep impression on him.

That hair of Matty's, that mass of beautiful, shining hair, which even his boyish, unpractised eye could see was something uncommon, — worth five dollars; it was impossible! And yet could it be? If "Jim's ladies" thought it so beautiful, it might be that it was worth a good deal of money. What fools, then, were Matty and Tony, the one for keeping it upon her head, the other for not persuading her to part with it, and taking a share of the money for himself! In all his life Theodore had never had so much money; and his mean, selfish soul at once set itself to devise means by which one — he did not yet, even to his own thoughts, say himself—could gain possession of the girl's hair.

He had heard of girls being robbed, in the street, of their hair; but that would never do here with Matty, no, not even though he had an accomplice to help him. And he knew of no one to whom he could even suggest such a thing; for he had no acquaintances in the city save the boys in his school; and to no one of them could he or would he dare to propose it, although he knew that there were among them some who were none too scrupulous to do a shabby thing if they thought they could gain any advantage by it.

All this time I had vainly, as I thought, tried to gain any influence over Matty. She took my gifts, it is true, and wore or otherwise made use of them; but she never showed the slightest token of pleasure in them, or uttered one word of acknowledgment, and she was still entirely unresponsive to any other advances on my part. It was Tony, bright, jolly little Tony, who thanked me with real Irish effusion, always greeted me with the broadest of smiles, and testified his gratitude and appreciation of my efforts for Matty's welfare by various small offerings, till I really wished I had chosen him to befriend instead of that hopeless subject, his sister. It became quite a little family joke, as almost every evening when he and Matty came to deliver the day's earnings to Jim — for it was not considered safe for them to carry the money to their own home — he brought also some small token for "Jim's second young lady," whereby I was understood; now a couple of daisies, a rose, or two or three violets, or a few sprigs of mignonnette, begged from Dutch Johnny; now a bird's nest, manufactured by himself out of twine and a few twigs; and once a huge turnip which he had seen fall from a market-cart as it passed on its way down the avenue, and picking it up, after vainly trying to make the carter hear, had laid it aside as a suitable gift for me; and another time he brought for my acceptance a hideous, miserable, half-starved kitten, which, as I was known by the servants to have a horror of cats, was declined for me both by Jim and Thomas, greatly to Tony's mortification and disappointment.

At the Easter festival, when he and Matty had "looked as good as anybody," to his mind, each child in the Sunday school had been presented with a small pot of pansies; and Tony, instead of taking his home, had come from the church to our house, and, asking for me by his usual title of "Jim's second young lady," had shyly presented his Easter token.

Yes, I would fain have made an exchange, and taken Tony as my charge; but pride, and the recollection of Milly's fear that I would not persevere with Matty, forbade.

I had thought over all manner of plans for removing both children from the influence of their wretched home and drunken parents; but most of these were pronounced by the more experienced to be visionary and not feasible. So they still continued to return to them at night, although, "weather fair or weather foul, weather wet or weather dry," they never failed to be present at their post as early as possible in the morning.

Miss Craven and I had taken from Jim the charge of providing the cripples' dinner; and for a

trifling sum Mrs. Petersen, who had no children
of her own, gave them that meal and their supper
in her room, so that in many respects they were
far better off than they had been.

But still there seemed no loop-hole where I
could insert a wedge for Matty's moral regeneration ; she appeared to remain hard, impenetrable,
and suspicious.

The story of the "ducking" had, of course,
been graphically rehearsed by those of the school-
boys who had witnessed it, to those who had not ;
and there were but few, if any, who did not enjoy
the recital of Theodore's punishment and disgrace. And from that time Captain Yorke had
become a marked figure with the boys. Before
this, he had not been known to many of them ;
but now he was pointed out by the few who had
been present at the scene at the fountain, as the
Spartan grandfather who had not hesitated to
deal out punishment to his own flesh and blood,
when it seemed to him that justice demanded it.
He was often to be seen now in the park, the
centre of an admiring and appreciative group, to
whom he related thrilling adventures which were
his own experience as a sailor and a surfman,
holding his audience spell-bound, not only by
their interest in the subject, but also by his quaint
and simple manner of telling.

Among this audience one day, were the two boys
who had been present at the theatre on the night

when the captain had made such an exhibition of himself; and they recognized him at once. Of course, it was soon spread about that he was the hero of that adventure; and the next morning at school, Jim was asked if he had not known it. Acknowledging this, it was then inquired *why* he had not "got even with Theodore," by turning the laugh on him, and telling that it was his grandfather who had made himself a laughing-stock.

"'Cause I wasn't goin' back on the old captain," answered sturdy, loyal Jim. "He's stood up for me, an' been a good friend; an' I ain't goin' to point him out for to be laughed at, not if he is Theodore's grandfather."

He expected to be laughed at in his turn, and stood with defiance and "laugh if you choose" in his air.

But no one laughed or jeered: somehow his steadfastness struck a chord in most of those boyish hearts; and Rob Stevens, clapping him on the shoulder, exclaimed, —

"And 'tain't the first time he's held his tongue, either, is it, Peanuts? We'll all vote for the feller that stan's by his friends an' don't go back on 'em. Three cheers for President Jim Washington!"

And if a voice there was silent, save Theodore Yorke's, it was not noticed in the number which responded.

School-life having by this time rubbed off some of his *freshness*, Jim had learned that it would be to his own advantage to discard several from the string of names which he had seen fit to adopt on his entrance; and he now contented himself with signing his name James R. L. Washington, which appeared upon all his books and any thing else to which he could lay claim.

After the manner of those who have fixed their minds upon that to which they have no right, the more the unprincipled Theodore thought of the mint of money, as he called it, upon Matty's head, the more he wished that he could find the means to possess himself of the material to be so easily turned into that money; and he finally arranged a plan which he thought both practicable and safe.

"Matildy Jane," whose theory it was that there were no articles of diet in New York "fit for plain folks to eat," and who believed that her father and mother would return home only to die victims to indigestion brought on by high living, had sent, by the hands of a friend who came to the city, a large basket of apple turnovers and ginger cookies, in order that her parents might have "a taste of home cookin'."

Slyly possessing himself of two of these turn-overs and sundry cookies, Theodore thought to make his peace with Tony and Matty by bestow-ing them upon them, as an equivalent for the stolen peanuts; and having ascertained when

Dutch Johnny was off on another purchasing expedition, and Tony left in charge, he hurried home, and came back to the florist's shop with these delectable viands.

No sooner did Tony see him than he warned him off, threatening to call the police if Theodore came any nearer; but the latter hastened to propitiate him by holding up the turnovers and saying, —

"Oh, I came to make up. Don't make a row."

Now, if there was any thing in which the soul of Tony delighted, it was an apple pasty of any shape or dimensions; and the tempter had unwittingly chosen his bait well.

Tony's threats and denunciations ceased, and he sat staring at the proffered treat; while Theodore, seeing it was taking effect, drew a few steps nearer.

"Don't you want 'em?" he said. "I've got one for you, and one for Matty; and I've got some ginger-cakes, too."

Warned by past experience, Tony grasped his crutches, and, still expecting some trick, sat dubious, with his eyes fixed as if fascinated upon the coveted dainties, but still more than half inclined to call to the policeman, whom he saw upon the upper corner.

"Oh, come now!" repeated Theodore; "make up. Don't you want 'em? They're first-rate."

The temptation proved irresistible; and, rising

to his feet, Tony went toward his whilom antagonist in order to prevent him from coming too near the stand, accepted one of the turnovers, looked at it on all sides, smelled of it, and finally set his teeth deliberately but with caution into it ; then turned, and looked inquiringly at Matty.

"Pisen !" uttered that little sceptic, still unconvinced that treachery did not lurk behind these demonstrations of friendship.

Ay, poison indeed! but not in the sense poor Matty meant. Nor would she accept the other turnover or the ginger-cakes, or look at or speak to Theodore; but sat gazing afar off as if into vacancy, her face perfectly expressionless, although Tony, now completely won over, sat eating his with the utmost gusto.

Meanwhile Theodore, having turned over the whole contents of his pockets, talked in a friendly way, leading gradually up to the matter in his mind; although he was afraid to linger long, lest Johnny should return, or some one come by who would wonder at seeing amicable relations established between himself and Tony.

"Been makin' good sales to-day?" he asked at length; but this put Tony on his guard again at once.

"Now you let peanuts alone ; they ain't none of your business," he said, his mouth full of ginger-cake.

"I ain't goin' to touch your peanuts," said the

older boy. "I just asked. Jim's makin' an uncommon good thing out of this peanut-stand with you and Matty to run it for him, an' I hear you're doin' first-rate. But — don't I know something about Jim!"

"So do I, lots," answered Tony, as well as he could speak.

"You don't know what I know; and Jim wouldn't want you to," said the bad boy. "It's his secret, and a monstrous one, too; but I know it, and I'm goin' to tell it, too."

"I sha'n't listen to it," said Tony.

"Ho! I don't want you to. It's not you I mean to tell," said Theodore. "It's the police."

"Jim ain't done nothin' for the perlice," said Tony furiously. "The perlice likes him, an' wouldn't do nothin' to him."

"Ha! You wait and see," said Theodore; "they've got to when I tell 'em. It's a secret on Jim an' one of his young ladies, Miss Amy there, that gives Matty her clo's an' things. He'll feel awful to have himself an' Miss Amy told on, and the police will go for 'em when they know it; but nothin' ain't goin' to put me off talkin' without I was paid for it, as much as five dollars, too."

"What they done?" asked Tony, curiosity and alarm for his friends getting the better of his aversion to discuss the subject with Theodore.

Theodore came nearer, and making Tony promise with the most solemn asseverations that he would not repeat, and would not suffer Matty to repeat, to any one, what he told him, said, —

"They had some poisoning done, round to Mr. Livingstone's, an' Jim and Miss Amy was mixed up in it. They did the poisoning; but 'twas found out in time, an' their folks hushed it up. But *I* know it, an' I'm goin' to set the police on them unless some one would make it worth my while not to. Five dollars would buy me off; but there's no one I know of, would give me five dollars, so I'm goin' to tell."

Street Arab though he was, with his wits sharpened into preternatural acuteness in some respects, in others Tony was guileless and easily imposed upon; and for a moment he stared at Theodore in dismay, but presently doubt and suspicion again obtained the upper hand.

"I don't take no stock in that," he said; "it's a lie, I know. I'll ask Jim himself."

"If you let on to him what I've told you, I'll tell the police for certain, whether or no," said Theodore; "but if anybody was to say they'd give me five dollars, an' you don't tell Jim, I'll never say a word."

And he walked away, leaving his words to take what effect they might. That they had already taken effect, he saw, as Matty, who had not spoken a word all this time, drew the beautiful, shining tresses in front of her, and passed her skinny little hands lovingly over them. Tony stood staring stupidly after him for a moment, then burst out at him with a torrent of abuse and threats which Theodore did not deign to answer.

That evening about dusk, when Tony and Matty came to our house to render up the day's account to Jim, after they had settled business, Tony asked in a mysterious whisper, and half as if he feared to put the question, —

"Jim, tell us; has you got a secret you don't want any one to know?"

By the light of the gas-jet, beneath which they stood, in the basement hall, Tony saw the color rush in a flood to Jim's face, and an angry light came into his eye, as he answered roughly, —

"'Tain't none of your business if I have; you let my secrets alone."

Tony was a little frightened, but he persisted, —

"But tell us; did you and yer young lady, her what's good to us, did you once get mixed up wid pisenin' some folks, an' it was kept dark so's the" —

"Now you shut up an' clear out quick, you little rascal!" shouted Jim furiously. "If you come Paul Pryin' round here, a-tryin' to find out my secrets, me an' you will fall out, an' you'll get no more help from Miss Amy nor me. Clear!"

But Tony, alas! was answered; and the crest-fallen little cripple shuffled out from the presence of the offended head of the peanut firm as fast as possible; Jim putting his head out of the door, and shouting after them, still in the most irate tones, —

"Now you let me an' Miss Amy an' all my folks alone, or there'll be trouble, sure!" then slammed the door after them.

In silence they went up the street, but not immediately home : they had other business to attend to first.

CHAPTER XII.

CAUGHT IN THE ACT.

CHAPTER XII.

CAUGHT IN THE ACT.

JOHNNY PETERSEN looked in surprise, consternation, and wrath when the two little cripples entered his shop the next morning, shamefaced and sheepish, as if they expected to be called to account for something.

And he did not lose time in making known the cause of his displeasure, could they, indeed, have had any doubt on that question.

Matty's hair was gone, cut close to her head, almost shaved off ; and the loss of it gave the poor little face a more wizened, pinched, and unnatural expression than ever. The effect was perfectly startling, and repulsive in the extreme ; and after staring at the child for a moment, and all but dropping the flower-pot he held in his hands, he broke forth into a torrent of words, mingling German and broken English in a manner which made them all but incomprehensible to the poor little ones. But they knew well enough what brought them forth, and they had no explanation to offer. It was their secret, and must remain a secret, so they thought, if the sacrifice were to be worth any thing.

Naturally, Johnny laid the blame of the transformation on the debased parents, whom he knew to be capable of any deed, no matter how shameful or cruel, if thereby they could obtain the means to procure liquor. Tony and Matty gathered, from the jargon which he sputtered forth, that this was his idea ; and they were quite satisfied to have it so, for no sentiments of filial affection moved them to enlighten him.

And it was not only the loss of that wealth of hair which made Matty look far worse than she had ever done before. She had not on the decent garments she had worn for some time past, but was in the ragged and soiled clothes which she had of late worn only when she went home at night, discarding them in the morning when she stopped at Mrs. Petersen's and put on the better ones which had been given to her. To all Petersen's questions she opposed a sullen silence; although she hung her head, and appeared embarrassed, which she was not apt to be.

But Tony, with his jolly little face clouded over, appeared really distressed, and looked from his sister to the florist and back again in a distraught, helpless sort of way, which quite touched the heart of the kind old Dutchman ; but neither from him could Johnny's rather incoherent questions draw forth any satisfaction, and the children both were glad when the entrance of a customer drew Johnny's attention for the time from themselves.

But the situation did not improve for the two little unfortunates when Mrs. Petersen, uneasy that they had not appeared at her rooms for the usual change of clothing, came bustling up to know if her husband could tell her any thing of them ; and, not a little astonished to find Matty at her post and Tony also at his, plied them anew with questions in English rather better than her husband's, and to which it was more difficult to avoid giving straightforward replies. But she gained as little as he had done, and she, too, took it for granted that either the father or mother had deprived the little hunchback of her hair.

The truth was, that the children had not cared to face her with the change in Matty's appearance, and hence had concluded to come to the day's business in their old clothes.

But Mrs. Petersen, energetic and stirring, was not going to let the matter rest thus, but was determined to probe it to the bottom if possible, and declared that she was going at once to see the mother, and call her to account. Whether she had some vague idea of bringing the supposed offenders to justice, or of restoring the lost locks to Matty, I cannot tell ; but just as she was leaving, Milly, Bessie, and I, bound for an early trip to spend the day with a friend in the country, whose birthday it was, came into the shop to purchase some flowers.

The morning was damp and chilly, although there was the promise of a fair day later on ; and Matty's stand was placed inside when we entered the shop, and the first thing our eyes rested upon was Matty's shorn head. We all three leaped at once to the same conclusion with the Petersens. But whether it was that I was more forcibly struck than the others with the cruelty of the thing, from having something of a fellow-feeling for Matty in the possession of a profuse quantity of hair somewhat like her own, although, as she had said, hers had been "purtier" than mine, despite the lack of the care which mine had always received, or that I had less self-control over my emotions ; certain it is that I burst into a passion of tears and sobs, which astonished not only the good florist and his wife, but also my own sister and friend. I was ashamed of them, but could not control them ; and perhaps it was as well that I could not do so immediately, for those tears made their way where all else had failed to effect an entrance; and, to my great astonishment, Matty seized with both her hands upon mine, which in my great pity and sympathy I had laid upon her shoulder, and, carrying it to her face, laid her cheek upon it. The next instant she dropped it, and sat looking down with the same stolid expression that she ordinarily wore. Indeed, it had hardly changed even at the moment of that most unusual demonstration, for no trace of any emotion had been visible on the worn, old little face.

Tony was delighted, as pleased as though his sister had given evidence of some wonderful talent, or performed some heroic action.

"She likes ye, miss," he exclaimed, "an' I allus knowed she did, though she wouldn't let on. She likes ye fust-rate, though she wor kinder back-'ard 'bout lettin' on. Now don't ye like the lady, Matty? If she hadn't liked ye lots, miss, she wouldn't er " — Here he checked himself with a frightened, embarrassed look, and rushing out of the little store, applied himself vigorously to the turning of his empty, fireless peanut-roaster.

But not a word, and not another token of any thing like feeling, was to be drawn from Matty. The rock had hardened again, and to all appearances no softening influences could be brought to bear upon it. It was not until Mrs. Petersen again expressed her positive intention of going to call the elder Blairs to account, and was about to start off for that purpose, that the child roused herself again, and turned, with something of apprehension in her expression, to look for Tony, who, having discovered that he was working aimlessly, was making ready to kindle his charcoal and fill his roaster.

"I go to dat mutter an' fader; I gif dem some pieces of my mi-int," said Mrs. Petersen, as she turned toward the door; but Milly stopped her.

"Do not, please, Mrs. Petersen," she said, in a tone too low to reach Matty's ear. "It will only make trouble for yourself and us. We cannot give poor Matty back her beautiful hair; and if you vex those dreadful people, it will only put fresh difficulties in the way of persuading them to give up the children."

"I tell dem my mi-int," persisted Mrs. Petersen; but finally she was persuaded to listen to reason and to satisfy herself with relieving her "mi-int."

My idea had been to induce Mrs. Petersen and Johnny — or Mrs. Petersen rather, for Johnny was sure to follow her lead, to take Matty and Tony under their care, and give them a home. Cousin Serena had offered to furnish the means for Tony's support, and I to do the same for Matty. But the florist and his wife had been unwilling to undertake the charge, even if the parents could be bribed to give up the children, lest they should be exposed to trouble in the future; therefore the Blairs had not yet been approached on the subject. I was for taking high-handed measures, and having the children separated from them on the ground of neglect and cruelty; but wiser and less impulsive heads than mine had decided that there was hardly sufficient reason for this, and I had been obliged to restrain my impatience and content myself with such alleviations of their lot as I could compass at present. I am not patient by nature, and could not bear to have any delay or hinderances put in the way of my schemes for the benefit of those children, and in secret I chafed a little over this.

It will readily be surmised what had become of Matty's hair.

Doubting the truth of Theodore's story, and yet fearing that there might be some foundation for it, Tony had confided to his sister that he meant to ask Jim about it, notwithstanding Theodore's warning to beware how he did so. Jim's anger at the questions he had put, especially at that regarding the "poisoning," had been enough to convince him that it was all true. Jim *had* a secret which he was afraid to have known; and that secret could be nothing more nor less than the alleged poisoning, which he plainly could not or would not deny; and which, according to ignorant little Tony's ideas, he was afraid to have come to the ears of the police. Theodore had learned of that unfortunate occurrence — as we heard later when all this came to light — through the medium of a stray copy of the objectionable paper containing the paragraph before referred to. This he had happened to read to his grandfather and grandmother, who, proud of his ability to do this far better than they could do it for themselves — for reading with Captain and Mrs. Yorke was a work

of time and difficulty, involving more pains-taking
than pleasure — often set him to amuse them in
this way in the evening.

"Madison Avenue" to Captain Yorke was com-
prised in the block on which our house was
situated; and the curiosity of the old man being
insatiable, he had never rested until he had located
the house. By dint of questioning Thomas and
the other servants, he soon learned all there was
to know, and was greatly excited and very wrathy
when he heard the truth. He repeated this to
his wife and grandson, bidding them never to say
a word about it, as the family had been much
annoyed and displeased. Theodore, however, had
once ventured to ask Jim about the matter, and
had been met by such a burst of fury that he
had never ventured to speak of it again to him.
Not for fear of offending Jim, however, but because
he dreaded the anger of his grandfather, should Jim
complain, as he threatened to do, to the old man;
for Jim would have told in this case on my account.

But it answered Theodore's purpose when he set
himself to work to devise means to obtain the five
dollars he coveted. He had aroused the fears of
these ignorant children for those who had been
kind to them, and having been convinced by Jim's
behavior that it was all true, Tony had proposed
what indeed had been in Matty's mind before, that
she should sell her hair, and so buy Theodore's
silence. Matty had agreed; and that morning,

before they had made their appearance at the
florist's, they had gone to a barber's, and, with
small worldly wisdom, Tony had demanded if he
would give five dollars for Matty's hair.

Gazing with astonishment and delight at the
mine of wealth displayed for his approbation, the
barber drew the long silky tresses through his
fingers, and closed the bargain at once, as well he
might, supposing him to be possessed of neither
heart nor conscience. Matty's head was expe-
ditiously shorn, and the proceeds of the unright-
eous sale were put into Tony's hands ; for he had
appeared as the speaking partner throughout the
transaction, Matty maintaining the usual impassive, sullen silence, so seldom broken save for her
brother and the Petersens.

The next thing to do was to see Theodore and
to hand him the money ; and being in haste to do
this before he should have time to give the dreaded
information to the police, Tony went to the board-
ing-place which was his home at present, Matty
waiting for her brother on the neighboring corner,
and asked for Theodore.

Now, this proceeding, as it proved, brought
swift detection and punishment upon the young
blackmailer.

Theodore had not remembered to guard against
the children coming to the house ; indeed, he had
not thought of his rascally scheme bearing fruit at
all so soon.

Happily for the frustration of that scheme, Theodore was out, having been sent on an errand by his grandfather; and the old captain himself, who was lounging on the front steps, was the one who first met the lame boy. Tony, who was not able to read numbers, had not been quite sure of his ground in the row of houses all so much alike; but he had no further doubt when he saw Captain Yorke.

At first he drew back, uncertain whether to make it known that his business was with Theodore; but his fear that his tormentor would "tell the perlice" before he had the opportunity to quiet him was too strong for his caution, and he asked the captain if Theodore was "to home."

"No, he ain't; an' what ye want with Theodore, sonny?" asked the captain.

Tony hesitated and fidgeted; and the old man asked sharply and quickly, "He ain't been hookin' your peanuts agin?"

"No—o," stammered Tony; and the captain, coming down the steps to where the boy stood, laid his hand upon his shoulder, and said sternly,— although the sternness was not for the cripple,—

"Ef he's touched another peanut, or been a-wrongin' of ye any way, tell me, — tell me right off. What is it?"

But Tony dared not tell; and the honest old seaman, whose confidence in his grandson had never been fully restored, was convinced that he had been about some of his evil ways again. He could do nothing with Tony, however; no persuasions could avail to draw any explanation from him; and he presently made his escape, hobbling down the street with the marvellous celerity with which he used his crutches, leaving the captain a prey to disquietude and apprehension.

Nor had he hope of obtaining any thing like the truth from Theodore himself: so he asked him no questions when he returned, nor did he tell him that Tony had come to ask for him, but, after taking counsel with himself, resolved to see Johnny Petersen, and tell him to be on the watch; and soon after we had left the florist's, he appeared there.

Tony saw the old Brutus coming down the street, stern and determined of aspect, trouble in every line of his weather-beaten countenance, and supposed himself to be his objective point. Dreading further catechism, and not being willing to encounter it, he dropped the crank of the peanut-roaster, and was off again before the captain was near enough to speak. Johnny could tell nothing, he thought, save that Matty's hair was gone, which the old man could not fail to see for himself; and his sister, he well knew, would not speak. For a moment he thought he would seize his opportunity, and hasten back to the house while Captain Yorke was away, and hand Theodore the five dollars; but he recollected that the oppressor would be at school, and so this would be useless. From a safe distance he watched for the captain's departure, and did not venture near his post till he saw him come out and walk away.

As he had foreseen, not a word could either Captain Yorke or the florist draw from Matty, when the former had made known the purpose of his coming; and they both questioned her closely. One might have thought that she was utterly deaf and dumb as she sat opposing that stolid, determined silence to all they said. Johnny knew nothing which could throw any light on the subject; and after telling him of Tony's embarrassment, and bidding him be on the watch, the heavy-hearted old man left the little shop.

Johnny did keep on the watch, but refrained from asking Tony any questions, keeping his eye upon him, however; but no further developments appeared until later in the day, when he saw Theodore coming down the other side of the avenue, and observed that Tony raised a warning finger to him as if to bid him keep his distance. Theodore paused on the opposite corner, and Tony went over to meet him.

Considerations of delicacy did not withhold Johnny from intruding upon what was evidently meant to be a private interview; and when, after a moment's converse, Tony put his hand in his pocket, and drew forth something which he gave to Theodore, the florist darted from his shop, and rushed across the street with an agility which was hardly to be expected from one of his years and girth.

Theodore saw him coming, and his guilty conscience leaped to the truth; Johnny suspected something wrong, and was coming to accuse him.

Closing his hand tightly on the prize which he had just received from his victim, he turned, and started to run. But an avenging Nemesis, in the shape of a piece of orange-peel, was behind him; his foot slipped upon it, and he came heavily to the ground. Before he could rise, the florist precipitated himself upon him with so much momentum, that he too lost his balance, and fell flat upon the boy. Not one whit disturbed was Johnny, however, by the fear that he might have injured his prisoner, although he had half knocked the breath from the boy's body; on the contrary, he would, I think, have been quite pleased to know that Theodore was seriously bruised.

Rising with some difficulty, and not without assistance from a passer-by who had seen the catastrophe, puffing and panting, but still retaining the hold he had taken of Theodore's collar, he hauled the boy to his feet, and, regardless of the punishment he had already inflicted, gave him a hard cuff upon the ear, saying, —

"You runs away from me, will you? I learns

you, my poy, you shtays ven I vants to shpeak mit you."

Supposing from this authoritative address that he was the father of the boy who had been guilty of some wrong, the man who had helped him passed on his way, leaving him to deal with the culprit as he saw fit. And Johnny saw fit to handle him with any thing but gentleness, pushing him before him across the street, and into the shop, giving him now and then a vicious shake, diversifying this with an occasional punch in the back with the fist of the disengaged hand. Had they had any distance to go, they would probably have drawn a crowd after them; as it was, they reached Johnny's quarters without attracting any special attention.

"Now," said the breathless florist when he had his captive safely within the shelter of the shop, "now, vat is your pusiness mit Tony? Tony is my scharge, an' I don' let him talks mit poys what shteals what don' pelongs to dem. Vat you got here?"

And he seized the tightly closed hand containing the five dollars, which Theodore had not yet found opportunity to conceal in a safer place. Theodore resisted; but he was no match for Petersen, who tripped him up again without compunction, and, regardless of consequences to the surrounding plants, — which happily came to no harm in the struggle, — sat upon him, and opened his hand with both his own.

Five dollars!

Johnny was not a particularly brilliant Dutchman, and his mind was generally slow in arriving at any conclusion; but the two and two which were to be put together here were not difficult to compute; and as he looked from the five-dollar bill to Matty's shorn head, and back again, he was not long in deciding that they made four. Matty for once showed some sign of emotion as she sat rubbing her hand over her poor little head in a nervous manner; although beyond this, and the stare with which she regarded the combatants, she showed no trace of interest in the affair, never once opening her lips.

"So!" said the florist, holding out the bill at arm's length, — "so! How is dis? You put Matty's head to de schissors, an' take him all off, und you shteal den her monish. De peanuts is a pad pisness; but dis is so much vorse as it goes to de prison. Tell me, Tony, how is dis?"

"I didn't steal it, he gave it to me; and I didn't touch Matty's hair," panted the prostrate Theodore. "He — he — he wanted me to do something for him, and he said he would give me that if I did it. Oh! let me up!"

"Hole your mout, and shpeak ven you is shpoken mit," said Johnny. "Tony, shpeak an' tell me. How vas it? You is cut off Matty's head; you is got de monish, five tollars, vat I tells you he is vort ; now tell me what for you gifs dis five tollars to dis pad poy, a poy so vorse as I do not know. I *vill* haf you tell me ; if no, I calls de police."

There was no escape ; on all hands Tony saw visions of the police, who would soon ferret out the whole matter, away back to Miss Amy and Jim (so Tony thought) ; and he found it best to throw himself and all concerned on the mercy of his old friend, and make a full confession.

As he told the shameful story of how Theodore had threatened to tell Jim's "secret," and to let the police know of the "poisoning" unless some-body paid him five dollars to keep it quiet ; of the confirmation he had himself received from Jim's manner and words when he asked him about it ; of how he and Matty had resolved to save their friends by the sacrifice of the hair which Johnny himself had often told them was worth so much money ; of how they had gone to the barber's, and sold the hair ; and lastly, how he, seeing Theodore on the opposite side of the street, had hurried over to bribe him with the five dollars to hold his peace, and how Theodore had accepted the price, — the kind-hearted florist waxed more and more angry ; and when he rose, and once more hauled the boy to his feet, it was only to seize a cane, and administer such a chastisement as the culprit had seldom or never received.

Theodore made little or no outcry, however, for

he was afraid of attracting attention from without, and perhaps himself falling into the hands of the law ; for he did not know, if his deeds were once made public, how far he might be under the ban of that authority.

"Now you go," said Johnny, when at last he paused, breathless from all his exertions, and with one final shake released his captive ; "go und tell de gran'fader I fin' vat is de matter out, und I gifs de vorst vips as I could gif to de vorst poy in all de down, und so I safes him some droubles. But if he dinks to gif you some more of de same veesic, I dink it not too moosh. For dat gran'-fader, I says notings to de police for dis time ; bud if you says one leetle more vord apout de young lady or dat goot poy Jim, or makes afrait any more dese schillens, den you see some dings to make you shtare. Go, go !"

And Theodore stood not upon the order of his going.

The pleasure of the day with our friends had been much marred for me by the recollection of the shorn head of my forlorn little *protégée* and the repulsive appearance she now presented ; and I was more than ever anxious to remove her from the father and mother, who, I thought, had treated her so unjustly and cruelly ; and I could not reconcile myself to the idea that this afforded no grounds for my taking them away.

But that difficulty was presently to be solved in

the most satisfactory way to those who had at heart the welfare of the crippled children.

Mother had occasion to send Jim upon an errand shortly after his return from school that afternoon; and he found it convenient, according to his usual custom, to return by a roundabout way, and stop at the peanut-stand. The excitement in Johnny's small establishment had hardly subsided when he made his appearance, and it was little wonder that he tarried long on his errand; so long, indeed, that mother rather lost patience, and said that she should forbid his stopping at his favorite haunt, except by express permission, if this occurred again. But his want of punctuality was quite forgiven when he came in with the tidings which he bore.

As usual, however, when any question arose of Theodore's want of principle, or any instance of it was shown, there was something in Jim's manner which excited the attention of those of the household under whose immediate observation he most came; and again Milly was surprised to see how wistful, uneasy, and absolutely nervous he was, appearing, as he often had before, as if there were something on his mind which he wished to tell her, but which he could not muster courage to confess.

CHAPTER XIII.

MATTY IS PROVIDED FOR.

CHAPTER XIII.

"OF course," said Uncle Rutherford, that evening in family conclave, "this business settles the question of that scholarship for Theodore Yorke. He has proved himself more utterly without principle or common honesty, than I could have believed possible ; and while, for poor old Yorke's sake, I should be glad to give him another chance of redeeming his character, I do not feel that the boy himself is worthy of it. He is radically bad and vicious, with a natural leaning toward deceit and dishonesty, and a capacity for crime that is absolutely startling, or he never could have arranged so deliberate a plan to obtain money from these poor little cripples. It was absolute blackmailing; and the Yorkes, I fear, have sad trouble in store for them with the boy. All the better for your *protégé*, Milly, if he continues to do as well as he has done lately. That fellow is in earnest, whatever may be the aims and influences which control him."

"I think," said aunt Emily, "that Mrs. Yorke is right, and that it would be best both for the captain and for Theodore to go home. The old man keeps her in a constant worry, by his very innocence and simplicity, which are so easily imposed upon ; and it will be far better for that boy to be where he is not surrounded by so many temptations. Do you not think so, Nicholas ? Better for him to be in his quiet, out-of-the-way home, than here, where there are so many inducements to evil for a boy without principle, such as has certainly proved himself."

Before Uncle Rutherford had time either to agree or dissent, Thomas announced that Captain Yorke wished to see Mr. Rutherford and Mr. Livingstone, and was told to show the old man into the adjoining library, whither papa and Uncle Rutherford adjourned to see him.

But through the half-drawn portières, the rest of us heard all that passed ; and, indeed, the captain was not reticent, — it was not in his nature to be, — and he would have been quite as garrulous in the presence of an audience of any size, provided he knew all his hearers to be friends. And not even the gravity of his errand, or the subject on which he held forth, could restrain him from the various deviations and wanderings to which he was prone when talking. It will not be necessary to repeat all these here.

The old man had gone back to Johnny Petersen's just as the florist was closing his shop for the night, timing his second visit after the hour

at which he knew the cripples would have left,
and asked Johnny if he had any further information for him. Johnny was not inclined to talk,
he found, and tried to evade his questions ; but he
was obliged to allow that Theodore had appeared
again ; and finally, so determined was the captain,
that he asked him to come with him to his home,
where he would tell him all.

Seated in Mrs. Petersen's cosey room, the poor
old seaman heard the story in all its details, half
bewildered by the good Dutchman's broken English, but fully able to extract from it all the painful and shameful particulars of his grandson's
rascality. Once launched into his narration,
Johnny spared nothing, and, at the end, rather
glorified himself for having taken matters into his
own hands, and administered condign punishment
to the culprit upon the spot ; nor did he deem it
necessary to apologize to the grandfather for having done so, neither did Captain Yorke seem to
expect this, or to think that he was not perfectly
justified in all that he had done.

Theodore had gone home, after his encounter
with Johnny, evidently suffering and much crestfallen ; but when his grandfather had questioned
him, he had added to his sins, and accounted for
this, by saying that he had had a fight in school ;
he being quite unaware of the captain's suspi-
cions, and of his interviews with Tony and the
florist in the morning. His grandfather had not

yet confronted him with the discovery of his sin ; for he had come directly from the Petersens to our house, deeming it best to take counsel with those whom he considered wiser and less interested than himself.

"I thought I had done with all sich work when I heered Tom was took," said the old man pathetically ; "but here it's broke out agin, an' me an' Mis' Yorke not so young as we was by a long shot, an' can't stan' it so well. The Scriptur says, 'Like father, like son ;' an' I've faith to b'lieve it, seein' I'm provin' it in my own fam'ly."

"No, no, captain," said uncle Rutherford, holding out his hand kindly to the veteran, "you must not say that, for if Tom had been like *his* father, he would have been a man in whom all who knew him placed confidence. And " — contradicting his own words spoken some time since — "we will not despair of your grandson yet. He is young, and under good influences now."

"It's all the wus, Gov'nor," said the captain, shaking his head, " all the wus to see him so young and so wicked. The Scriptur' says, 'The ways of transgressors is hard ;' but I b'lieve the ways of them what has to do with the transgressors, an' foller them up, is harder, an' them's my opinions."

Father and uncle Rutherford each offered a few words of sympathy, and endeavored to comfort him ; but he was not yet to be consoled, and could see no hope for the future. He was terribly distressed over the necessity of telling Mrs. Yorke, and said that he meant to "sleep over it," and think of the best way of breaking it to her. But we all knew how much probability there was of that. No sooner would he see his wife, than his full heart would overleap all restraint he might have intended to put upon it, and she would be put in possession of all the facts, down to the smallest details.

In the midst of his own perplexities, however, the captain did not forget a piece of news he had brought with him, and which especially interested me, and speedily drew me into the library.

While he was still with the Petersens, but on the point of taking his leave, the sound of crutches had been heard on the stairs ; and Johnny, turning to listen, said, —

"Dems is Tony mit his crushes. Vat is upper now?" and opened the door to admit not only Tony, but also his sister. Tony was flustered and frightened, with eyes half starting from his head ; but Matty was impassive as usual, and showed neither terror nor excitement.

"They've gone !" exclaimed the lame boy.

"Who are gone? Vat is de madder?" asked Johnny ; then added, before Tony could answer, "Poor leetle poy, he is all upside down mit dis day. Shpeak, Tony."

"They've gone," repeated Tony ; "an' what is

wus, the furnitur' is gone too, an' there ain't no beds nor nuthin'."

"Vat is gone?" asked Mrs. Petersen in her turn; then, jumping at her own conclusions, added, "De vater an' de mutter?"

"Yes, and good riddance, too; on'y we ain't got any place to sleep," said Tony; which filial sentiment found an echo in the hearts of all present.

It was all true, as Johnny found on investigation. When Tony and Matty had gone home that evening, they found the wretched room on the top floor of a tenement-house, which they had inhabited with their father and mother, empty and tenantless; the few articles of worthless furniture (if furniture it could be called) which it had formerly held, taken away. But if there was no one there to welcome them, neither did there await them the abusive language and hard blows they too frequently encountered. They were not in the slightest degree troubled by the loss; their only feeling seemed to be, as Tony expressed it, that it was a "good riddance," save that they had no other resting-place for the night. A pitying neighbor had given them their supper; and they were told that their mother had gone out early in the morning, soon after they had gone to business, and, re-appearing with a carter, had had her few possessions carried away, leaving no word whither she was bound, or message for the helpless children. The mystery was solved in a degree, when two police-officers appeared a few hours later, saying that Blair was "wanted" for a grave offence against the law; but the bird had flown, and so far left no trace.

I was delighted, and could almost have thanked Blair for committing a crime which rendered flight necessary, and seemed to leave the way open for a decent provision for the destitute children.

Captain Yorke told us that Mrs. Petersen was going to keep them for the night, and that they were already quite at home and comfortable, and Tony excitedly happy, — happiness and Matty could not be associated, — with the motherly German woman and her husband.

But our two gentlemen and Captain Yorke had not yet come to any conclusion as to what was to be done with Theodore; and it was an embarrassing question to decide. To take the boy, a boy who was making fair progress in his studies, and who was pains-taking and ambitious, from school, and bury him in the quiet sea-side home, where, save for three or four months of the year, he would be almost altogether cut off from association with any but the few still primitive inhabitants of the Point, and where he would be entirely deprived of any advantages of education, seemed almost too much punishment even for the grave offences which those three honorable, high-minded men found it hard to condone. But, again, it was not to be thought of, that, devoid of conscience and right feeling as he was, he should be left alone exposed to the temptations of the great city. For Captain and Mrs. Yorke must shortly return home, Mrs. Yorke's physician having pronounced her sufficiently cured to be allowed to do so in the course of a few weeks; and, even as it was, the nominal protection of Theodore's grandparents had formed no safeguard against evil. The evil was in his own heart, but he might be placed where there would be fewer opportunities for its development.

It was a grave matter for consideration, and could not be hastily decided.

"Of course," said uncle Rutherford, as he bid the captain good-night, "of course it is out of the question for Theodore to remain in the city after you and Mrs. Yorke leave, even under the care of the kind woman with whom you now board; he would not recognize her authority, and would consider himself free to go any lengths. No, that is not to be thought of; but we may devise some other plan by which he may have some schooling and be kept in proper restraint; and he may yet in time prove a help and comfort to you, Yorke. For your sake I would do much to set him in the right way; and his teachers think that he has the making of a clever man in him, if we can but instil something like principle into his character. Take heart, man."

But the captain went out sadly and hopelessly

shaking his gray head, over which twenty years seemed to have passed since the morning of that day.

It was not, perhaps, that his affection for his grandson had been so deeply grieved; for the boy had, until less than a year since, been quite a stranger to his grandparents, and Theodore was not an attractive boy even to his own family; and, had the choice been given to the captain, he would undoubtedly have much preferred to claim Jim as his own, his open, sunny, joyous nature responding much more readily to the old man's than did that of the far less amiable Theodore. But he felt ashamed and disgraced, and as if he could not bear to look any one of the name of Rutherford or Livingstone in the face, while he still felt that to our family alone could he turn for help and advice in this sad business.

"Ye see, you and Mr. Livingstone knows a heap more 'bout wicked ways an' doin's than me an' Miss Yorke does, Gov'nor," he said to uncle Rutherford, altogether innocent of any uncomplimentary inference which might be drawn, "an' so ye'd know the best ways out of 'em. Yes, I says to myself, says I, if there's enny one knows the ways out of a bad scrape, it'll be them city born and bred gentlemen; so I come along to tell ye afore I tole Miss Yorke or nothin'. Mebbe ye could tell me how to make it a little lighter for her," he added wistfully.

Alas! beyond the promise to think the matter over, and to consider what was best to be done, his two friends could give him little consolation to convey to the poor grandmother, who had built so much on the opportunities offered to the boy who she had hoped and believed would prove a credit and support to the declining years of herself and her husband.

The next morning, directly after breakfast, I announced my intention of going immediately round to see cousin Serena, and asking her to go with me to Mrs. Petersen's, to ascertain if there were any hope that she would take Tony and Matty, now that their father and mother had apparently deserted them. I would provide for Matty, and cousin Serena wished to do the same for the boy. I was very eager now to carry out my plans, believing that the lions in the way were entirely removed, and that no one could have any further objection to my doing so.

But, to my great disgust, again there were dissenting voices; for father and mother, aunt Emily, yes, and even impulsive, push-a-thing-ahead uncle Rutherford, said that it would not do to take it for granted that the elder Blairs would not return and claim the children. It was not probable, they agreed, but it was more than possible; and all my elders were quite positive that the Petersens would not undertake the care of Tony and Matty until they felt assured that the parents were not likely to meddle with them, or to make trouble for those who had them in charge.

"But I want to go and see," I said, determined, if possible, to carry my point at once, "if the Petersens *will* do it — and they may. There is no use in leaving Matty unprovided for. What will she and Tony do if Mrs. Petersen will not keep them while it is uncertain whether that man and woman return or not ?"

I spoke in rather an aggrieved tone, feeling somewhat inclined to think my relatives hard-hearted.

"Interview Mrs. Petersen, if you choose, my daughter," said papa; "only be prepared for disappointment."

"I only want to see Matty provided for, papa," I answered, a little ashamed of my former pettishness.

"And Matty, and Tony also, shall not be allowed to suffer, Amy," said uncle Rutherford sympathetically; mindful, perhaps, of his own propensity for forcing things to a wished-for conclusion at once.

"I'll see cousin Serena, and take her views, anyway," I said, my good humor restored; and I lost little time in carrying out my purpose.

Miss Craven herself was so eager and earnest when in pursuit of any plan, especially when it was for the benefit or pleasure of others, that I built much on her co-operation in the work of persuading the Petersens to take the cripples under their protection at once; and I was proportionately crestfallen when I found that she took the same view of the case as my own family, saying also that she did not believe that Johnny and his wife would agree to my proposal, and that she did not think it advisable that they should. However, she willingly consented to go with me to the Petersens.

And, lo! I returned triumphant; for Mrs. Petersen, moved probably more by the utter desolation of the children than by any arguments or persuasions of mine, had consented without difficulty to take them for the present, and to retain them so long as the parent Blairs did not return or claim them.

And whatever his wife decided, that was sure to be the best in Johnny's eyes; so, her consent being gained, there was no fear of a dissenting voice from him. Moreover, recollections of his own youth inclined Johnny's heart to be merciful.

"Und why for no," he said, when appealed to on behalf of the deserted children, "why for no? Sometime ven mine fader und mutter die mit me, und dere vas nopody to gif leetle Johnny notings, vat should he do, if did not come some goot peoples vat take und eat him und sleep him? I don' forget; und how I vas done py, I do mit der oders. Mine wife she vas so goot as a mutter for dem."

The arrangement was concluded to the mutual satisfaction of the Petersens and myself, to say nothing of that of Tony, — Matty, as usual, showing no sign either of pleasure or the contrary. There was no time lost in settling the cripples in their new quarters, so superior in all respects to any they had ever enjoyed before. There was nothing to be moved from those they had occupied with their father and mother ; not a splinter, not a shred, beyond the clothes they had on and those kept at Mrs. Petersen's, was left to them ; indeed, had there been, we never should have allowed them to claim it, nor would Mrs. Petersen have allowed it to come into her tidy apartments.

My day was occupied in a fever of energy, running from one place to another, providing beds and clothing and other articles, — many of which, had I not been checked by wiser counsels, would have been unnecessary and unfit, — dragging cousin Serena with me ; begging from mother, aunt Emily, and Mrs. Sanford, and drawing somewhat heavily on my own resources. At last every thing was ready, to the serene content of Mrs. Petersen, who now seemed to feel as if she had really adopted the children ; and when evening came, I rested in the happy consciousness that Matty was at last well provided for, as I would have her, and that I had carried my point with comparatively little trouble.

Jim beamed upon me every time he came near

me, and he appeared to have a sense of partner-ship which was not a little amusing.

Amy had "taken it awfully hard," my brothers, Norman and Douglas, said as they ran me on my new burst of philanthropy; but I was too com-placent and well satisfied to be at all disturbed by their comments.

Little did I dream, while dwelling on the future I had planned for the little hunchback, that a higher hand than mine was so soon to take all provision for her into its own keeping.

On the afternoon of the next day, as Milly and I, just dressed for a very different scene from that to which we were suddenly called, were passing down the stairs to the carriage which was await-ing us, Jim came rushing up in a state of terrible excitement, with distressed, frightened eyes look-ing out of a deadly white face.

"Miss Milly! Miss Milly!" he gasped, all out of breath as he was with rapid running, and ad-dressing first the one to whom he was accustomed to turn in all emergencies or need for help, "Miss Milly, oh, come quick! No, no — it's Miss Amy I mean. Miss Amy, come quick; she wants you!"

"Who wants me? what is the matter?" asked both Milly and I in one breath, and very much alarmed as we saw that there was really some serious trouble.

"Matty! She'll be gone, miss. Oh, come

quick!" he answered, still in the same breathless manner.

Visions of the drunken mother returning for the child, and striving to take her away against her will, at once presented themselves to my imagination ; and now, indeed, my boasted interest in Matty was tried. Was I expected to face this worthless, angry woman, and rescue my poor little *protégée?* I could not do it ; this was my first thought. Then, again, was I to abandon the poor child without one struggle, without one effort to prevail on the woman to leave the helpless child in the better hands into which she had fallen ? Like a flash of lightning all this passed through my brain ; then I said to Jim faintly and with a faltering heart, —

"Is there any one there to help ?"

"Yes, miss," answered Jim ; "there's Johnny, an' Mrs. Petersen, an' the policeman brought her in, an' the doctor. But, O Miss Amy, do make haste ! she wants you so bad, an' the doctor said to bring you quick."

The doctor ? Then was Matty ill, in danger ?

"What is it, Jim ? Do speak," said Milly. "What *is* the trouble ? Is Matty ill ? do you mean she is dying ?"

"The doctor said so, Miss Milly. 'Twas the fire-engine. But *do* be quick !"

A sickening horror came over me, and Milly turned as white as a sheet ; but no more time was lost. We hurried into the carriage, bade Jim mount beside the coachman, and, not even knowing whither we were bound, left the directions to him.

But the drive to our unknown destination was not a long one; and in two minutes we drew up at Dutch Johnny's little flower-store, around which a crowd had gathered, through which we had to push our way; or rather the policeman, who stood by the door, opened a way for us.

Stretched upon the floor, in the midst of all the delicate verdure and brilliant color in the florist's small store, lay Matty, her little shorn head supported upon the breast of Mrs. Petersen, who was bending over her with the tears running down her cheeks. At Mrs. Petersen's side was Tony, leaning his head against her other shoulder, his face a mixture of terror, grief, and bewilderment, both his hands clasping those of Matty; around were grouped Johnny, a doctor, and a second officer.

Matty's eyes were fixed upon the door; and as we entered, a sudden gleam of intelligence and pleasure lighted them. She drew one of her hands from Tony's clasp, and stretched it out to me.

Regardless of my light spring costume as it came in contact with the damp floor of the greenhouse, I knelt in front of Mrs. Petersen, and bent over the poor little creature. Only once in my life had I seen death; and then neither my affections nor my sympathies had been enlisted, and my sensations, from the nature of the circumstances, had been only those of horror and repulsion, and I had fled from the sight, while now the recollection of it was as some dreadful dream. Never before had I seen a soul pass from the one life to the other; but countless experiences could not have told me the truth more forcibly than did the look upon the face so small, so pitifully old and care-worn. The hand of God's angel had already written it too plainly there.

A merciful angel, blotting out the traces of suffering and weariness and oppression such as, happily, few of God's little ones are called upon to bear; and imprinting in their place rest and peace unspeakable.

For Matty was passing away without pain; the injuries she had received had dulled sensation, while they were destroying life.

She motioned for me to bend down, for she was almost past speech; then raising both hands she tried to push back my hat. I flung it aside, and she passed her hands over my hair again and again, and drew her thin fingers, from whose touch I did not shrink now, through the curling rings about my forehead and temples; then her lips moved, and Tony stooped to listen.

"She says hers 'more purtier,'" said the poor little brother, half choking.

"Yes, Matty," I said, "much prettier. You had the prettiest hair I ever saw." Then, as a sudden inspiration flashed upon me, "I am going to that barber to buy back your hair, Matty; and Tony shall have it for his own to keep all his life."

Her face brightened, and a smile, the first, the only smile I ever saw upon it, lightened it and almost transfigured it; then she turned her eyes from me, and looked around the little store till they rested upon a beautiful pink azalea which stood at a little distance, — beautiful in itself, but not for the purpose for which Matty wanted it.

Taking one hand from my hair, while the fingers of the other still lingered among my curls, she pointed to the plant, and looked wistfully at Johnny. The good German was not usually quick of comprehension; but he understood the mute appeal now, and he asked in a voice even more husky than his usual guttural tones, —

"Vat you vants, Maddy? Some dem vlowers?"

She nodded assent, and the florist hastily cut a cluster, and put it in her hand. With fast-failing strength she tried to place it in my hair; but the effort was too much; and Milly, who stood behind me, assisted her to arrange the blossoms as she would have them. A look of intense satisfaction passed over the pallid face, as though to her untutored taste this glaring adornment was all that could be desired; then the hands fell, and the lips moved.

Both Tony and I tried to hear; but the only word I could hear was, "suffer."

"Do you suffer so, poor little Matty?" I asked, for the doctor had assured us that she did not.

She shook her head feebly, and I heard the word "children."

"What children? Do you mean you want to see my little sisters, Matty?" I asked.

"No, miss," interposed Tony. "I knows what she means. It is a teks was hung up in the Sunday-school room right forninst where she sat, an' she used to sit starin' at it like she hadn't nothin' else to think on; an' the lady what run the class teached it to her one day, 'cause it was the Golden Teks for that day, an' she's made me be a-hearin' ov it a many times since. She did set sich a heap by that teks as I niver saw, an' I'm thinkin' she wants yer to be a-repeatin' of it to her, miss. — Does yer, Matty?"

Again she nodded; and I said as well as my sobs would let me, "Suffer little children to come unto me, and forbid them not; for of such is the kingdom of heaven."

"More, more," she whispered faintly; and I repeated over and over again the sweet, gracious invitation which has lasted and shall last through all time, gathering into those loving arms the little ones of every degree, the beautiful and the uncouth, the happy and the oppressed; until to the echo of that golden text poor Matty's soul floated away peacefully and quietly.

Unsightly, unhappy, and unloved, save for the

faithful young brother to whom she was all in all, — to her, little had been given ; and we may surely believe that from her little would be required.

So was Matty provided for, and the care of her taken from my hands and those of generous Jim, who really seemed to mourn for her as though she had been his own sister.

The particulars of the circumstances which led to her death, as related by Johnny Petersen, Tony, and the policeman who had witnessed the accident, — for accident it was, — were these.

Matty had had the most unbounded terror of the fire-engines, — perhaps owing to the fact, stated by Tony, that her deformity had been occasioned by her being thrown from a window during a fire when she was a very young child ; and she probably associated the engines with all the misery, both mental and physical, which she had ever since suffered. However that may be, the sight or sound of them was sufficient to rouse her from the state of dull apathy usual to her, into a paroxysm of alarm and nervousness ; and if Tony were any-where within reach she always sought his side with some fancied idea of protection, until the terror was beyond her vision and hearing.

Tony had been sent by Johnny on some errand, and was returning, and had nearly reached the opposite corner of the avenue, when the sound of the galloping hoofs and rattling wheels of a fire-engine were heard.

Matty at her stand without the florist's shop was out of harm's way; but no sooner did the clatter of the approaching steamer strike her ear, than she hastily rose from her seat, and started to meet Tony, who, pausing with boyish interest to watch the engine as it came up the cross street, did not 'see or heed his sister until it was too late. Johnny saw from within the shop, and started to hold back the child: but fear lent wings to Matty's usually slow and faltering footsteps; she heeded not or heard not his calls; and, before he could reach her, the engine swung around the corner into the avenue, and the already so sadly disfigured little form lay among the trampling hoofs and crushing wheels.

Johnny himself had raised her, and carried her tenderly into his little bower, where he laid her down among the flowers to breathe away the few short moments of her waning life. Seeming to be conscious at once of what was before her, she had made Tony understand by signs and one or two faintly gasped words that she wanted me; and Jim, who had as usual stopped in on his way from school, had hastened to bring me.

Sobered and sadly impressed, and yet with a feeling that Matty's release was a blessing beyond all expression, Milly and I returned home, with no heart, as may be supposed, for the entertainment for which we had been bound when we were called to her.

CHAPTER XIV.

JIM'S CONFESSION.

JIM'S CONFESSION.

Two days had passed, and poor little Matty had been laid to the rest which knows no breaking; and all about Mrs. Petersen's rooms and the little flower-shop had settled to its usual routine, save that Tony still abode with the kind Germans, and that he tended alone both the peanut-stand and his roaster. His parents had not yet returned, nor have we to this day obtained, or indeed sought, any trace of them; all concerned being only too glad that they have made no claim upon the little lame boy. Tony, now no longer a peanut-vender, has been promoted to the post of assistant and errand-boy to Johnny Petersen, who, with his wife, treat the lad as if he were their own son, instead of a little deserted waif cast by a merciful Providence into their kind hands.

I had, happily, — or rather Edward had for me, — been able to rescue Matty's beautiful tresses from the hands of the conscienceless barber, who, when approached on the subject, demanded the most exorbitant price for them; but finding that the circumstances of the first sale were known to the gentleman, and being confronted with Tony, whom my brother had taken with him and left outside till he should ascertain what advance in price would be asked, he came down in his demands, and parted with them at exactly three times the sum he had paid for them, and which probably, in righteousness, he should have given to Matty.

They were at once given to Tony, whose pride in them had been only less than that of his sister, and who, with a show of tender sentiment scarcely to be expected from one of his surroundings and antecedents, received them as a gift from the dead. Cheery, jolly little Tony! but for this and other similar tokens of an affectionate heart, it might have been thought that he was wanting in feeling, so easily did his elastic, joyous spirit throw off trouble; so completely did he extract all the sweet, and throw aside all the bitter, offered to him by a lot in life which most of us would not have envied.

In the trouble and excitement over the sudden fate of the little "deform," as Allie and Daisy had called her, we had for the moment put aside the question of what was to be done with Theodore Yorke; but now it was to be decided.

That the boy could be touched; that he was not lost to all trace of human or decent feeling, — was shown by the trouble, and, his grandparents thought, remorse, which he testified on hearing of Matty's tragical death ; and he would even have tried to make some amends to Tony, had not the lame boy absolutely refused to let him come near him ; while the florist, seeing him from within the shop, rushed out upon him, and threatened him with some more of the same "veesic" as he had administered before, seeming inclined to do so whether or no ; and Theodore, plainly thinking discretion the better part of valor, had lost no time in putting a safe distance between himself and the pugilistic old German.

Not wishing to discuss the subject in the presence of the culprit or his distressed and anxious grandmother, uncle Rutherford had told Captain Yorke to come again to our house in the evening of the day on which Matty was buried ; having first taken counsel with father and mother and aunt Emily as to the best course to be pursued for all interested. The captain seemed quite to have lost his usual independence and courage, and had put himself and his family into the hands of those who he knew were good friends to him and his.

"I didn't let on to the boy, Gov'nor an' Mr. Livingstone," he said, rubbing up his grizzled locks as was his wont when talking, "I didn't let on to the boy as we was thinkin' he was to be took from school ; but I'm glad to say he was consid'able cut up along of that poor little hunch-back, an' his bein' so mean to her jes' afore she was took; an' I'm thinkin' he has some kind of feelin's in respecks of her, all the more mebbe as he thinks he's goin' to get off 'thout any more punishment than what he got; an' I don't bear no grudge agin that Dutch flower-man for what he done to him, — an' isn't he a Dutchy though! 'Pears like he ain't never studied no grammar nor good English, nor nothin', an' them's my opinions. He do talk the funniest, an' mos' times I don't hardly make no sense of it. But," with a heavy, long-drawn sigh, "what was yer both of ye thinkin' it was bes' to do?"

"We have thought, captain," answered uncle Rutherford, to whom father left all explanations, "we have thought it would be best and wisest, if you and his grandmother and mother agree, to send Theodore to a boarding-school on Long Island, where he will be kept under very strict discipline and supervision."

"Supervision! an' what may that be, Gov'nor, askin' yer pardon?" said the old man, as uncle Rutherford paused for a moment to see how he would take his proposal.

Uncle Rutherford explained, and, seeing that he must confine himself to simple words, went on, —

"We know the gentleman in charge, and believe that he will have an especial eye to Theodore if we ask him to do so; and he is an excellent teacher, and will bring him on in his studies. If

Theodore does well there for a year or two, and shows himself fit to be trusted, we may then remove him to a different and higher school, where he may still fit himself to be a man, and a help and comfort to you. He has his future in his own hands; let him do well, and Mr. Livingstone and I will see that he is provided for till he is fitted to take care of himself; but an opportunity which might have been his " — O, dear uncle Rutherford, why need you have told this? — "must pass to another who has better deserved it. Do you feel that you can part with the boy, and let him go to boarding-school?"

"I reckon I ain't goin' to have much feelin's agin it," answered the captain, whose face had assumed an expression of intense relief as uncle Rutherford unfolded his plans. "I don't set such a heap by the boy as to set my face against his goin' to the boardin'-school, if it do be stric'; it'll do him good; an' he ain't got roun' me so's the other gran'children have, an' I'd a sight rather we had Jim for a gran'boy than this one, if he is my own flesh an' blood, as they say. I ain't never took no stock in him sence the first day he come, when I see him take his little sister's bigger cake unbeknownst to the little one, an' put his'n what was not so big in its place."

There were no family secrets or shortcomings which would not come to light when the captain was on the high-road to such disclosures; for a

wise and discreet reticence was not his distinguishing characteristic, as we know.

"I hope he'll do well, an' turn out a credit to
ye, Gov'nor an' Mr. Livingstone," he continued, as
though washing his hands of the boy, though all
the while the trouble dwelt upon his weather-
beaten old face; "but *I* bet on Jim, an' I wish it
was him had the chance ye speak of. Mebbe it is,
now; an' if it was, it'd be 'most a set-off agin
the other not havin' it. I set a lot on Jim!"

And the old man looked inquiringly at uncle
Rutherford, who was not, however, *quite* so indis-
creet as his interlocutor, and kept his own counsel
so far as this.

So it was settled, then. Theodore was to be
removed from the school he was attending at
present, and sent to the boarding-school, where
he would be under far closer restraint than he
could be in the city, or even at home with his
grandparents; and there could be no question
that the old man felt that a great responsibility
was taken from his shoulders.

"I wish it was time to go home. I mean, I wish
Miss Yorke was cured up so's we could go home,"
he said. "I reckon I've seen about all there is to
see in this town; an' it's my opinions I might
'bout as well be thinkin' of the scines an' poles,
an' lobster-pots, an' so on. Course they wants
lookin' arter 'cordin' to custom this time o' year;
an' Jabez he's took so to carpenterin' an' what he

calls cabiny-makin', he's goin' to let 'em slip, Jabez
is ; an' come time for settin' 'em they ain't goin'
to be ready, an' I reckon I oughter to be there ;
but the doctor, he says four weeks more for Miss
Yorke, an' he'll let her go cured. She's pretty
first-rate now, an' she don't walk no more with a
cane, on'y comin' up an' down the stairs. I never
did see such folks to have long ladders of stairs as
York folks is ; when I fust come, I used to think I
wouldn't never get to the top of 'em ; an' even the
poor folks here has to go a-pilin' theirselves up
atop of stairs as high as a mast, one lot atop of
another. Ye get up near the sky there ; not that
folks is so good an' heavenly ; no, no; there's on'y a
few of 'em that way ;" with an approving nod at
father and uncle Rutherford, and a comprehensive
wave of his hand, as if to say that he excepted
from his adverse criticism both of his present companions, and all who belonged to them ; "on'y a
few; but they're pintin' straight for the New Jeru-
sylem," — another nod pointed the compliment.
"Where was I ? Oh, them stairs. Wa'l, as I
was a-sayin', I reckon I've had 'bout enuf of 'em,
an' I'd like to be home where I can be down onto
the flat groun' an' not like to what's his name's
coffin, what I heerd the boys speakin' about, what
got hitched half way up to heaven an' stuck there.
He's a fable feller, ov course ; Mahomet, that's
his name ; there ain't never been no such doin's
sence miracle days 'cept in the theayters an' them

places.   An' t'other night Miss Dodge, she asked
me would I go to the opery, an' I says 'yes.'   I
was boun' to see all there was to see, an' we went;
an' such a goin' up stairs as there was there, up
an' up an' up, an' when we got there I thought
we might ha' stopped sooner; for down below
there was lots of folks sittin' an' standin', an' I
asked Miss Dodge why she didn't stop onto some
of them floors, three or four of 'em below, an'
she kinder smirked, an' says it costs lots to go in
there.   Wa'l, I couldn't make out what they was
at on the platform, — the play actors; it wasn't
half so nice as the mother-in-law actin'; they did
all their talkin' to singin', an' they died singin',
an' all sorts of things; an' there was a old man
got young an' fell spooney on a girl; an' they
all got foolisher an' foolisher, an' the devil was
there, an' such a mix-up; an' bimeby the girl, she
died in a prison, an' angel actin' folks come down
an' took her up, — leastways was takin' her up to
heaven, — an' there come a hitch, an' there they
stuck, half up, half down.   Miss Dodge said there
must ha' been somethin' wrong with the machin-
ery what h'isted 'em; an' it made me think of
that feller's coffin, so I sung out, 'Mahomet's
coffin!' an' the folks, some larfed, they was mostly
boys an' young fellers, an' some few below looked
up; an' Miss Dodge, she was awful affronted, an'
she says she was glad enough we wasn't below,
she would ha' been too mortified.   W'al, that ain't

nothin' to do with Miss Yorke, for she wasn't along; she couldn't ha' clumb so high; an' I never was a man of many words, so I'll get to my p'int. As I was a-sayin', Miss Yorke, she can't go home yet, an' she can't be left alone, so I've got to stay on."

Here mamma went to the rescue; for, as before, the rest of the family were gathered in the next room, and heard all that had passed. The two gentlemen had allowed the captain to ramble on, partly because he amused them and us, partly because they knew it was of little use to try to stop him after he had once started to expound his views on men and things.

"Captain," said mamma, joining the two in the library, "Mrs. Rutherford and I thought you were growing weary of the city, and wanted to go back home; so we have arranged a little plan which may suit you both, and will certainly suit me well. I have a great deal of sewing to be done now, which I should like to have done in the house, and Mrs. Yorke is such a beautiful seamstress that I should be glad of her assistance. Suppose that she comes here. I can give her accommodation on the basement floor, so that she need not go up and down stairs; and Mammy and my own seamstress will gladly do all that is needful for her. Then you can go home as soon as you choose. Will you ask her?"

The captain gazed for a minute into mother's

face, then looked from her to father, from him to uncle Rutherford, and drew a long breath.

"Wa'l!" he ejaculated, "when you folks gets histed to heaven, I reckon there ain't goin' to be no hitch in the histin'. An' them's my opinions."

Having delivered himself of these "opinions," he rose, shook hands with mother, father, and uncle Rutherford, a long hard shake, expressive of his feelings; came into the room where the rest of us were gathered, and went through the same ceremony all round; returned to the library and repeated it, then once more back to the drawing-room for a second pumping of each arm, and finally managed to convey himself away; the last words which father heard as he closed the door behind him being, "No hitch in *that* histin'."

Two days after, Mrs. Yorke was comfortably settled in our basement, and industriously plying her needle; the captain was on his way home by water, where he would not be apt to go astray; while at a very few hours' notice Theodore had been removed from the one school, and sent to the other.

"Miss Milly," said Jim, meeting my sister in the hall on the afternoon of the day on which he had learned that his rival had been taken from the school they had both attended, and speaking in evident but repressed excitement, "Miss Milly, they say Theodore Yorke has left school for good. Has he, Miss Milly?"

"He has left your school, and been sent to another, Jim, where you will not be likely to meet him soon again," answered Milly.

"And they say it's an awful strict school, Miss Milly, a kind of a bad-boy school, where a feller don't get half so much chance as he does in ours."

"I think the discipline is very strict, Jim," replied his young mistress.

"And," wistfully, "he was sent there because of what he done — I mean, did — to Matty?"

Even in the midst of excitement, Jim was becoming careful to correct himself when he lapsed inadvertently into any inaccuracies of speech.

Milly hesitated for a moment, but she thought that the lesson might possibly point a moral, and she answered, —

"Yes, for that especially, Jim. It was his crowning offence; but Theodore is not a good, upright boy, and it was thought better to remove him to another and a stricter school."

"Thank you'm," said the lad as he walked away with a crestfallen air which much surprised Milly. Was he going to take so much to heart the absence of the boy between whom and himself there had waged a constant state of warfare ever since they had first met? Amy must be right, thought Milly, and there must be something behind these singular moods of Jim's. Was it possible that he, too, had fallen into temptation

and sin, and, seeing with what consequences these
had been fraught for Theodore, was now trembling
for himself? She could hardly believe this, Jim
had proved himself so frank and upright; but
there must be something which he was hiding,
and this was the only solution at which she could
arrive.

But she was not kept much longer in doubt.

Jim slept over the matter upon his mind and
conscience, and the next morning, which happened
to be Saturday, and therefore a holiday, came to
her, and requested a private interview.

The request was readily granted; and, taking
him aside, Milly waited with more anxiety than
can well be appreciated by those who did not
know her interest in the boy.

"Miss Milly," he said, shifting uneasily from
one foot to the other, and twisting his hands
nervously together as he stood before her, "Miss
Milly, I've got something I ought to tell you."

"Well, Jim?" said Milly encouragingly.

"I don' know what you're goin' to think of me,
miss," he answered with a very shamed face.

"If you have done wrong, Jim, and are ready
to confess it now, I shall not be very severe with
you, — you know that, Jim," said Milly. "You are
in some trouble. I have seen for a long time that
you had something on your mind; if you tell me,
I may be able to help you out of it."

"I ain't in no scrape, Miss Milly, if that's what

you mean," said the boy; "only — only — it's a mean kind of a thing, an' I've got to tell. 'Tain't fair for me to keep it to myself any longer. Bill's the only other feller knows. It's going to take my chance, for sure; but all the same, I've got to tell. I ain't so afraid of you as of — some others." He paused again, and again Milly had to re-assure and encourage him, bidding him remember that others as well as herself had his good and interest at heart, and that he had already tested these and not found them wanting.

"I know, Miss Milly," he answered, "but I can't bear for you or none of the family to think me a sneak, an' that's what I feel I've been now. 'Twasn't fair, an' now I know it. I did know it all along, on'y I wouldn't let on."

"Well, come, Jim," said Milly, determined to bring him to the point without any more of this shilly-shallying which was exceedingly unlike Jim; "you must tell me at once if you wish to do so, for I have an engagement, and shall have to leave you very soon."

"Well, miss," he replied, thus urged, "I found out — don't you be ashamed of me, Miss Milly — I found out about how Mr. Rutherford was goin' to give a big thing, some kind of a thing in the way of eddication, to me or Theodore Yorke, whichever turned out best this year at school, an' how he thought Theodore was a sneak, an' me too hot-tempered, an' always ready for a fight, — an' how he was goin' to see which did the best, not on'y in his learnin', but in his conduck, quite without us knowin' about what was afore us, an' then give that one this big thing. And, Miss Milly, you an' Mr. Rutherford, an' the rest of the fam'ly, maybe, thought me doin' well, an' takin' care of my temper. An' maybe so I was; but it was 'cause I was *bound* to beat Theodore, an' not let him get that prize. I felt awful mean all along; but now Theodore's cut up so, an' got sent off, an' he never knew nothin' about it, or maybe he'd done better, an' I don't feel it's fair in me. I knew, an' he didn't. I stood a lot from Theodore, an' didn't fly out at him on'y once or twice that you know about; but I wouldn't ha' stood it, an' there's many a time I would ha' fought him an' the other boys, too, on'y for thinkin' of that. So, you see, I did get more chance at the beginning than him, an' 'tain't fair in me. An' I thought to myself, If you're goin' to do a mean thing like this to get a hitch in life, how you goin' to get fit to be President? If you see somebody doin' a sneaky or dishonest thing, you can't have the face to pull him up an' send him to prison," — as may be seen, Jim's ideas of the Presidential authority were that it was unlimited and autocratic, — "when you know you got there yourself on the sly; an' I wouldn't feel fit for it. So there wasn't no comfort in it one way or another; an' I made up my mind I'd tell you, an' you can tell Mr.

Rutherford; an' anyhow I'll come out fair an'
even chances with Theodore. Mr. Rutherford
will maybe think this is worse than fightin' an'
blowin' out?" interrogatively and wistfully.

Milly had let him go on without interruption
when she had once succeeded in starting him, and
had asked no questions; now she said, —

"I think, Jim, that Mr. Rutherford will be
pleased that you had so far the mastery over yourself that you would not take what you considered
an unfair advantage over Theodore. I am glad,
truly glad that you have succeeded in learning to
control your temper; but still more glad that your
sense of honor and right led you to tell of this.
But how did you learn of Mr. Rutherford's plan?"

Jim related how Bill, overhearing the conversation, or at least a part of it, on the evening on
which the matter had been discussed by the family,
had been the medium of communication, and how
they had both resolutely guarded their knowledge
of it until now; when Jim had told his comrade
that he *must* make confession, and put himself, as
he thought, on equal ground with his antagonist
and unconscious rival.

"I didn't do it for no good feelin' to Theodore,
Miss Milly," he added, "for I b'lieve I just *hate*
Theodore. I didn't feel none too good to him ever
since first I seen him, an' the more I saw him the
worse I got to like him; but all the same, I'd got
to be fair to him when it come — came — to his

chance bein' lost. If I couldn't take care of myself that way, I ain't goin' to be fit to take care of
these United States. Miss Milly, you'll tell Mr.
Rutherford? I could tell you, but I couldn't
tell him."

Milly answered him that she would be the bearer
of his confession ; and left him, much relieved herself to find that he had been guilty of nothing
more serious, and thankful from her very heart to
see that her teachings and his newly-awakened
sense of justice would not allow him to take unfair
advantage of another, even though that other
might be one whom he considered an enemy.
She lost no time in seeking uncle Rutherford,
and telling him all, so that the boy might not be
in suspense longer than was necessary; for she
well knew that he would find a lenient judge in
our uncle.

Nor was she wrong. Uncle Rutherford sent for
Jim, and taking the boy's hand, shook it heartily,
as he said, " My boy, you have gained the mastery
over yourself, and no man can achieve a greater
victory. I could wish that you had tried to keep
control over your temper from a better and higher
motive than the wish to outstrip Theodore ; but
we may trust that you will set that before yourself
now. Go on as you have begun, and the scholarship is yours in good time. My best wishes go
with you, and I sincerely trust that you may win
the prize."